A POWER BOYS ADVENTURE

The Mystery of
THE
DOUBLE KIDNAPPING

By Mel Lyle

Illustrated by
Raymond Burns

WHITMAN PUBLISHING COMPANY • Racine, Wisconsin

Scott Stockbridge

Contents

The Mystery of
THE DOUBLE KIDNAPPING

1   *"Barry Donovan, Millionaire"*

The taxi stopped in front of the Lincoln, an apartment hotel on Lexington Avenue and 35th Street.

Mr. Thomas Power got out first, carrying luggage. He drew a deep breath of the clear morning air. It was eleven o'clock on a Sunday in July.

"It's always exciting to be here in New York," he said.

Now his older son, Jack Power, climbed out, and then his younger son, Chip, holding the leash of their Dalmatian, Blaze. The dog shook himself, his ears flopping. Chip stroked the dog's neck.

"Airplanes and taxis are not for dogs. Poor Blaze," Chip said. "But now you'll be able to stretch out and take a nice long snooze."

Blaze stood wagging his tail as Mr. Power paid the cab driver.

A doorman helped with the bags, and then Mr. Power signed the register at the hotel desk.

"Did our trunks arrive?" Mr. Power asked the desk clerk.

"Indeed they did, Mr. Power. They're upstairs in your suite."

"And the provisions I ordered?"

"All upstairs. And you're well stocked, if I may say so, sir. Enough food for a week."

"Well, I've got a couple of growing sons—with hearty appetites."

"And a very handsome dog," the desk clerk said.

Blaze barked in appreciation.

"Thank you," Mr. Power said.

The desk clerk rang for a bellboy.

"Gee, this is beautiful," Chip said in suite 903. He took off Blaze's leash and collar, and the dog ran about from room to room, inspecting. So did Chip.

There was an attractive living room, a bedroom for Mr. Power, a bedroom for Jack and Chip, and a dining room connected to a large kitchen.

Back in the living room Mr. Power said, "Hungry, Chip?"

"No, Dad. Are you?"

"Afraid not."

Chip grinned. "We all ate like horses on the plane."

"Tired, kid?" Jack asked.

"A little bit. Not too," Chip said, and then he scoffed. "Kid! I'm fifteen, he's seventeen—so I'm the kid."

"Oh, all of a sudden you're sensitive," Jack said.

"Well, if I'm a kid, what are you?"

"Boys, boys," Mr. Power said, smiling.

"Well, if you're not *too* tired," Jack said, "you

can help with the unpacking."

"Where's Blaze?" Mr. Power inquired.

Chip pointed. Blaze was asleep under a chair.

They all showered and changed clothes, and Mr. Power shaved.

When he had finished shaving, Mr. Power went to the telephone, and Jack said to Chip, "He's calling Mr. Donovan."

"Barry Donovan, millionaire," Chip said irritably. He *was* tired from the long trip, although he hated to admit it.

"That's why we're here," Jack said.

"I know why we're here," Chip said. "Mr. Donovan is the head of Donovan Advertising Agency. His office is in the Empire State Building. He lives on Thirty-second Street, just east of Fifth Avenue. He has a job for Dad—publicity for Pan World Airlines. Dad is going to do a human-interest photo story about the planes and the passengers for one of the big picture magazines."

"You should be proud," Jack said. "Your father was selected because in his own way he's a great man, quite famous as a free-lance photojournalist."

"Okay, I'm proud."

"That's why we're here."

"Okay, I *know* why we're here."

"No, I don't mean here in New York—I mean here at this hotel."

"Okay, *why* are we here at this hotel?"

"Because it's convenient. It's within walking distance of both Mr. Donovan's home and office."

"As if I didn't know. Boy, seventeen-year-olds must really think fifteen-year-olds are strictly dumb."

"Dumb," Jack said, laughing, "but not strictly strictly."

Chip threw a sofa pillow. Jack ducked. Mr. Power, hanging up the telephone, caught the pillow one-handed.

"Nice catch," Chip applauded.

"We're all invited," Mr. Power said.

"Invited?" Jack asked. "Where?"

"To Mr. Donovan's house. He wants to meet and greet my family. He's got a son your age, Jack."

"Good," Jack said.

"Family?" Chip asked. "Does that include Blaze?"

"Of course," Mr. Power replied.

Blaze, upon hearing his name, came out from under the chair, wagging his tail. He was ready to go visiting.

They walked along the sunny streets, Mr. Power and Jack in front, Chip lagging behind with the sniffing, inquisitive Blaze. Chip found himself idly studying his father and older brother as he walked. They were both so tall, he thought—although he himself was almost as tall. Mr. Power was dark and sturdy, his hair shot through with gray; Jack was slim with short-cut red hair, freckles, and serious green eyes. Chip himself didn't look like either of them. He was blond with blue eyes that people often called mischievous.

And now he and Blaze caught up with them in front of the brownstone house on 32nd Street. It was five stories high.

"You mean he has this house all to himself?" Chip asked.

"Not all to himself," Mr. Power replied. "He has a family. Remember?"

"How many are there?" Chip questioned.

"Mr. Barry Donovan; his wife, Sylvia Donovan; and their son, Dick."

"And just for those three they need this whole big house?"

"There are servants," Mr. Power said, "and there's a chauffeur, and there's Mr. Donovan's personal secretary."

"They live here, too?" Chip asked.

"I don't know about the servants," Mr. Power answered. "But I do know that the chauffeur and the personal secretary have separate apartments for themselves right here in the house."

"Gosh, it must be wonderful to be a millionaire."

Jack bowed to his brother. "Would you like to have the honor of ringing the millionaire's bell?"

Chip bowed in return. "I would love to have the honor. Okay, Dad?"

"Go right ahead, Son," Mr. Power said.

Chip rang the bell and they waited.

The door was opened by a tall, slender man. He was dressed in a black suit, a white shirt, and a black tie. He had a long, pale face, and brown hair parted in the middle. Chip could not see his eyes.

The man's eyes were covered by dark-tinted glasses.

2　　　*Two of a Kind*

"I'm Bruce Updyke, Mr. Donovan's secretary," the slender man said. "You are the Power family, I expect?"

"That's right," Mr. Power said from behind Chip.

The man smiled. He had good teeth. "Actually, I know because of the Dalmatian. Mr. Donovan told me there would be a Dalmatian."

"His name's Blaze," Chip said.

"Won't you please come in?" Mr. Updyke had a thin, high-pitched voice. Chip wondered what color the man's eyes were behind the forbidding dark-tinted glasses.

They followed Bruce Updyke through a wide vestibule. He opened a door, let them pass through, and closed it behind them, remaining outside.

They were in a huge living room which contained three people.

"I'm Barry Donovan," one of them, a chubby man, said. He was bald with a rim of white hair. He had a pink, round face and merry blue eyes. "And this is my wife, Sylvia," Mr. Donovan said, "and my son, Dick."

"And these are my sons"—Mr. Power gestured to each of them—"Chip and Jack Power."

Everybody shook hands.

"And Blaze," Chip added.

"What a lovely dog!" Mrs. Donovan declared. "Is he friendly?"

"Oh, yes," Chip said.

"May I pet him?" She was a beautiful woman with red hair.

"He'd love it," Chip said.

Gently she rubbed Blaze behind the ears, and

Blaze's tail waved like a flag. Then Mrs. Donovan said, "Is there something I can get you folks? Coffee, Mr. Power? Cokes for the boys? Or milk and cookies?"

"No, thank you," Mr. Power said.

"Nothing, thank you," the boys said in chorus.

"Then I shall gracefully retire and leave you men alone." She went out of the room, softly closing the door.

"Now then . . ." Mr. Donovan said, leading Mr. Power to a desk where they sat talking. The three boys and Blaze were gathered in another part of the large room.

Chip kept looking at Jack and Dick. He could not get over how much alike they looked—it was an amazing resemblance. Dick Donovan was tall and lean and red-haired, just like Jack. His hair was cut short, and he even had freckles. They looked like twins.

"You fellows going to stay in New York for any length of time?" Dick Donovan asked.

"It depends," Jack said, "on how long my father's work keeps him here."

"You fellows travel a lot with your dad?"

"Since Mom died, yes," Jack said. "Whenever we're on vacation, we go where his work takes him." He grinned. "We sure see a lot of the country. Dad travels a lot in his business."

"Your dad is a photojournalist, isn't he?" Dick asked. "That sounds like interesting work."

"Sure is," Chip put in. "Jack and I have all kinds of adventures traveling around with Dad." He yawned. He was tired. It had been a long trip coming in to New York.

"Where's home base?" Dick asked. "Where do you live?"

"Chicago," Jack told him. "The Windy City."

Chip sat in an easy chair and Blaze stretched out near him on the soft Oriental rug. Chip removed Blaze's leash and held it in his lap. He could hear Mr. Donovan saying to Mr. Power:

" . . . I would like you to go out to Kennedy Airport today, as soon as possible. Sunday's a good day —many people travel. You could finish that part of the job—the Kennedy Airport part—in one day and night. Then you can do La Guardia late this week, and next week the Newark Airport. Today's a good day for Kennedy because Mr. Ramsay Lee is in charge on Sundays, and he's a very good friend of ours. He'll cooperate with you fully."

There was a knock on the door.

"Come in," Mr. Donovan called.

Bruce Updyke entered with another man. The other man was very tall, blond, and broad-shouldered.

"Is there anything further you would wish, Mr. Donovan?" Bruce Updyke asked.

"No, I don't think so, Bruce," Mr. Donovan replied. "You've all met Mr. Updyke, my secretary?" he inquired.

"Yes, we have," Mr. Power said.

"The other gentleman is Mike Cheever, our chauffeur."

Mike Cheever nodded and smiled. He had a square face and narrow eyes and strong-looking teeth.

"Sunday is their day off—Sunday and Monday," Mr. Donovan said. "But if you'd like Mike to drive you out to the airport, Mr. Power . . . ."

"Oh, no, I wouldn't impose on Mr. Cheever on his day off," Mr. Power said. "I'll manage to get out there, thank you."

"All right, then, Bruce and Mike," Mr. Donovan called to them gaily. "Relax, enjoy yourselves, have fun. And do check in with me now and then."

"Yes, sir," Bruce Updyke said gravely. "Good-bye, all."

Updyke and Cheever went out. Mr. Donovan said, "Nice men, those two—rather new employees. I used to have Ben Thompson—served both as secretary and chauffeur. But he retired four months ago. Then I got Updyke as my secretary, and he recommended Cheever as chauffeur. They've been excellent, I must say."

Mr. Power approached the boys.

"Duty calls," he said. "I've got to go to work. I'm going back to the hotel for my cameras and things. So, if you're ready—"

"Oh, no!" Mr. Donovan interposed. "Leave the youngsters here. I'll provide an entertaining day for them, I assure you. They certainly know their way back without you, don't they?"

"It's up to you, boys," Mr. Power said. "Whatever you like."

"We'll stay, if it's all right with you, Dad," Jack said.

"Of course it's all right with me," Mr. Power said.

"Gosh," Dick Donovan said. "I'd be awfully disappointed if you dragged them away now, Mr. Power."

"No dragging, Dick. Nothing even remotely like that. I'm not that kind of father."

"You just leave everything to me and don't worry." Mr. Donovan smiled his merry smile at Thomas Power.

"All right?" Mr. Power asked his sons.

"Sure, Dad," Chip said.

Mr. Power waved good-bye and made his exit accompanied by Barry Donovan.

A maid came in with a tray of Cokes, milk, and cookies. She set the tray on a table, smiled at the boys, and went out again quietly.

Dick Donovan drank a Coke. Jack nibbled on a cookie and washed it down with cold milk. Chip felt a yawn coming on and suppressed it. He was not hungry. To tell the truth, he was sleepy.

"There's a real keen game at Yankee Stadium today," Dick Donovan said. "The Yankees and the Minnesota Twins. Dad and I were going—"

Mr. Donovan returned and picked up the conversation just where Dick had left it. "I've a couple of box-seat tickets for the ball game. I was going up with Dick"—he chuckled—"but it's my hunch Dick would prefer the company of people more his own age. How about that, gentlemen?"

"Well, now, Dad . . ." Dick began.

"I appreciate your effort at politeness, Son, but truth is truth." Mr. Donovan laughed. "Would you substitute for me, please, Jack?"

"Well, sir, I'd love it."

"Done!" Mr. Donovan exclaimed. "And as for you, Mr. Chip—I think that with a little effort I can scare up another ticket."

"No, thank you, sir," Chip said. "I'm—well, I'm a little bit tired. It was a long trip coming in. . . ."

"I understand," Mr. Donovan said. "Well, if you change your mind, there's still plenty of time. Just let me know. And now, gentlemen, with your kind permission, may I withdraw?"

"That's my pop," Dick Donovan beamed. "Thank you, Dad."

"I'll go visit with my wife now," Mr. Donovan said.

The boys sat around for a while getting acquainted and chatting amiably, and then Dick looked at his watch. "What do you say, Chip?"

"No, thanks." Chip stood up and attached Blaze's

leash. "I'll take a walk with Blaze back to the hotel, and then I think I'll turn in for a good long nap."

"We'll get together later," Dick said.

"Sure thing," Chip said. "Enjoy the ball game. I know you will."

"Good-bye, Brother," Jack said. "Don't take any wooden nickels."

"Don't you," Chip said and smiled.

Outside, the sun burned down. It was hot. The weatherman had predicted rain by evening, but it did not look like rain now. The sky was clear and the sun was a ball of fire. Blaze strained at the leash as they walked easterly.

The streets were quiet and deserted. New York was supposed to be a busy town, but no town was busy, Chip decided, not even New York, on a Sunday.

On the corner of Madison Avenue there was a drugstore open, and suddenly the desire for an ice-cream soda became imperative. Chip went in and found that he was the only customer in the store.

There were only himself, the man behind the counter, and a man enclosed in the single telephone booth, and no one else. Chip climbed up on the stool.

"What'll it be?" said the man behind the counter.

"A black and white," Chip said.

The soda, topped by a blob of whipped cream, was delicious.

Chip paid with a dollar bill, then realized that was all the money he had. Did Jack have money? Maybe. Chip hoped Jack did, but even if he did, Jack would be gone most of the day. Dad would be gone, too, according to the conversation he had heard —all day and most of the evening. He had better call right now to tell Dad to leave money in case of emergency—if Dad was still at the hotel. He collected Blaze and went to the phone booth.

The man was still inside the one phone booth, talking. Chip waited impatiently. He could see him through the glass door. He was a dark, burly man with a flat nose and black, bushy eyebrows.

Finally the man hung up and hurried out.

Chip went in, called the hotel, and asked for suite 903.

Blaze sat like a doll outside the booth.

There was no answer from 903. Dad was gone.

Chip hung up, swung open the door—and then saw the wallet on the floor.

Quickly he looked for the flat-nosed man. He was no longer in the store. Chip picked up the wallet, took Blaze, and rushed out.

The street was empty—no sign of the flat-nosed man.

Chip sighed and pocketed the wallet. He would inspect it when he got back to the hotel. There would probably be some sort of identification in the wallet, and he would call the flat-nosed man from the hotel.

Chip and Blaze walked slowly in the heat of the day. Blaze stopped once at a fire hydrant.

3 *Kidnapped*

While Chip was walking, Jack and Dick were talking.

"How will we go?" Jack asked.

"Well, we can either take a taxi or the subway," Dick said.

"I'd prefer the subway."

"Most people wouldn't," Dick laughed. "Especially on a hot day."

"You've got to remember, I'm a stranger here," Jack explained. "To me the New York subway is something of an adventure. You know how it is with us foreigners."

"Sure," Dick said.

"I mean—if you'd rather go by taxi . . . ."

"Actually, the subways are quicker. We'll go by subway, and you'll have your adventure. You'd better take this, though." Dick gave Jack one of the tickets his father had given him.

"Why are we splitting the tickets?" Jack inquired with a puzzled expression.

"Because sometimes the subways are crowded," Dick informed him. "We might get separated. Also, up at the Stadium there's going to be a crowd today. Big game. So also, up there we could get separated. This way, with you hanging on to your own ticket, we can't get lost. You'll be shown to your seat—just in case."

"I get it," Jack said.

"You're a smart fellow, Jack Power." Dick playfully punched at Jack's arm.

"No, really, you're being the smart fellow. I mean separating the tickets. Smart."

"Let's go," Dick said.

They paid their respects to Mr. and Mrs. Donovan and went out into the brilliant sunshine.

"Hold it!" Dick exclaimed.

"What now?" Jack asked.

"Forgot my binoculars. And I have an extra pair for you. Got to go all the way upstairs for them. Mind waiting?"

"Of course not," Jack said.

"Good boy. You pound the sidewalk. I'll be with you in two shakes."

"Well, more than that."

"Two minutes, then."

Dick turned, used his key, opened the door, and went into the house.

Jack went down the stairs to the sidewalk.

There was a car parked at the curb with a flat-nosed man in the driver's seat.

"Hey!" the flat-nosed man called.

Jack went near. The flat-nosed man came out of the car. There was no one nearby.

"Can't get the motor started." The flat-nosed man

had a deep, rasping voice. "Maybe you can give me a hand."

"Ignition trouble?" Jack asked.

"Maybe you can help me, young Donovan." The flat-nosed man opened the rear door.

"I'm not—"

Jack never finished the sentence. He saw something golden flash in the sunshine. For the one moment before he became unconscious it looked like a fountain pen. Then it was under his nose and he heard the hiss. He heard nothing more.

He went limp, and the flat-nosed man caught him.

Quickly the flat-nosed man pulled him into the car, straightened him into a sitting position on the rear seat, emerged, and slammed the door shut. He ran around to the front, got into the driver's seat, shut that door, turned the key in the ignition, and the motor purred. Smoothly and silently the powerful car pulled away from the curb. The entire incident did not take more than sixty seconds.

When Dick Donovan, carrying two pairs of binoculars, came out of the house, there was no sign of a car and no sign of Jack Power. "Now, where in the world. . . ."

Dick searched up and down the street in bewilderment.

4 *Telephone Calls*

At the hotel, in suite 903, Chip yawned, then released Blaze from the leash. Immediately Blaze found a comfortable corner, curled up, and went to sleep.

Chip grinned. "You and me both, Blaze," he said. "Sleepy. But me, all of a sudden I've got a responsibility." He slowly took the wallet from his pocket.

It was a fat, brown leather wallet. It contained money, a lot of money, all twenty-dollar bills. Chip whistled softly. There were at least fifty twenty-dollar bills. One side of the wallet had a cellophane window through which an identification card could be seen. Chip read to himself: Frank Bristol, 203 West 72nd Street. And there was a phone number: TR 2-9970.

Chip sighed, yawned, then made his way to the telephone.

Just as he touched it, as though he had pressed an invisible button—it rang. Startled, Chip pulled his hand back. The phone rang again. Smiling sheepishly, Chip extended his hand and picked up the receiver.

"Hello?"

"Chip?"

"Yes, this is Chip."

"Dick Donovan here."

"Hi," Chip said.

"Is Jack there?"

"Jack? He's with you. Or isn't he?"

"I left him outside," Dick explained, "and went back into the house to get binoculars. When I came down—no Jack."

Chip laughed. "Well, that's my brother for you."

"You mean," Dick asked, "this has happened before?"

"Well, maybe not this—but *things*. I mean, with Jack, things happen. Like adventures, you know? He's—what's the word?—*impulsive*. Maybe he met somebody."

"Or maybe," Dick said, "he went up to the ball game without me."

"But why in the world would he go without you?" Chip asked.

"We split tickets. I mean, I gave him his own ticket, just in case we happened to get separated. Maybe he misunderstood and went up alone."

"Could be," Chip said. "So you'll see him up there. If not, don't worry. If he had to go off somewhere, I'm sure he'll call you and tell you just what it was all about."

"I won't be back till practically evening. It's a doubleheader." Dick sighed. "Well, okay. Either I'll see him up there, or he'll call me, or I'll call him.

Thanks, Chip. 'Bye, now."

They both hung up. Chip was not worried. He knew his brother. Jack *was* impulsive and things *did* happen to Jack—all kinds of adventures. Always curious and eager, Jack perhaps *made* them happen to him, but Chip was not worried, because Jack Power, of all people, knew how to take care of himself.

Suddenly Chip realized he was still holding the wallet.

He looked again through the cellophane window at the identification card and dialed the number. He could hear the buzz as the phone rang at the other end. No answer. He hung up and tried again, counting. He let it ring ten times. No answer. He hung up and yawned.

He went to his bedroom and found that Blaze was trailing him sleepily. Chip removed his clothes, put on his pajamas, and stretched, feeling the relaxing pleasure of the long stretch. Then he put the wallet on the table beside the bed, got into bed, and pulled a thin blanket over himself. He turned and made the phone call again. No answer. He pulled up his knees and closed his eyes. There was a thump on the bed and Blaze was with him, and Chip could feel the comfortable warmth of Blaze's body beside him.

Within minutes they were both asleep.

Jack Power opened his eyes, but he could not see. For that one bewildering moment as he returned to consciousness, he thought he was blind. Then, as he gradually came to his senses, he understood why he could not see. He was blindfolded.

Nor could he shout. He was gagged.

Nor could he move freely. His wrists were bound behind his back, and his ankles were tied tightly.

He was lying on his right side on a cold, hard floor.

He rested like that, waiting for his mind to clear and his strength to return. Then he twisted up into a sitting position. He pulled his heels toward him on the floor, thus raising his knees. Now he lowered his head to his knees and worked the blindfold against his knees until finally it fell free.

Now he could see, at least.

He was in a large room with a high skylight. Through the skylight he could see it was late afternoon. There was no more sun; dark clouds hung heavily like omens of evil. Just then the clouds opened and the rain poured down.

Sounds of voices came to him from the next room.

He strained to hear over the insistent patter of the rain on the skylight.

A voice said, "You'll cut out newspaper type. You'll paste the words on a sheet of paper, and you'll arrange the note exactly as I've written it."

Despite the distance between him and the voices in the other room, despite the walls that separated him from them, and despite the interference of the rain knocking on the glass of the skylight, that voice, somehow, sounded vaguely familiar, but he could not place it. He was in a condition of shock, bewildered, frightened, still bound and gagged. And now he heard a second voice replying.

"Don't worry. I know what to do."

And now there was a third voice, a rasping voice. "Look, you guys don't need me anymore. I'm going home. Okay?"

And now the vaguely familiar voice came again. "I'm leaving, too. All right?"

"Sure. I'll be sleeping here."

"Take care of him. Don't forget to feed him. We don't want him dead. We haven't even gotten a look at him. Frank brought him in and locked him away. You sure he's all right, Frank?"

"He's okay." Frank's was the rasping voice.

"All right. Let's go."

And so the rasping voice and the vaguely familiar voice disappeared, and Jack was left alone with the man who would feed him and who would be sleeping there.

There were no more voices. Just shuffling sounds. Many shuffling sounds.

6 *Escape*

Sitting, bound, gagged, but with his strength having now returned and with his mind sharp and clear, Jack inspected his prison, his eyes roving to every nook and cranny. The room appeared to be a storage room. There were many ancient crates and wooden boxes, but what attracted his attention was an old steel cabinet in a corner. It was rusted and broken, and he knew why it was out of the way here in the storage room. Anywhere else it would be dangerous because of its sharp, jagged metal edges.

Sharp, jagged metal edges!

Carefully, slowly, twisting painfully, inch by inch, he moved his body along the cold, hard floor toward the steel cabinet. The noisy hail of rain on the skylight was a blessing. It covered any sound of his careful, sliding, twisting journey to the battered steel cabinet.

And then he was there, his back to the cabinet, his neck turned as he peered over one shoulder. He adjusted the bonds of his wrists to a sharp edge of steel and rubbed, up and down, cautiously, until finally the steel knifed through *and his hands were free!*

He sat motionless, listening. No one had heard. He breathed a prayer of relief.

Now, quickly, he removed the gag from his mouth and untied his feet. He stood up, wobbly. He leaned against the cabinet, waiting for his blood to return to normal circulation.

Then he moved. On tiptoe, lightly, silently, he went to the door.

The phone in the other room rang. Jack froze.

The man in the next room answered the phone. "Yes, yes," Jack heard him say impatiently. "I've got it done; I'm finished, all done." There was a pause, and then he continued. "Yes, I wore gloves— no fingerprints." Another pause, and then, "I'm going out right now to mail the letter. After I mail the letter, I'm going to a restaurant and eat. I'm starved. From there I'll bring back some food for him. . . . Okay. Good-bye."

Jack remained exactly where he was, stiff, motionless, waiting. He heard the footsteps going away, and then a distant door slammed.

And then there was silence. He knew he was alone in the house now.

Now!

He tried the door, turned the knob, and pushed. The door stayed firm as a rock. Locked. Of course!

He had time and he was not afraid. The man had gone out to mail a letter, and then he was going to eat. There was time, plenty of time.

He moved back several feet and hurled himself against the door. He was strong. He hit the door like a battering ram. The door shuddered, but it held.

He moved back, hunched a shoulder, and hit it again, and again and again, in powerful rushes like a football tackle. The door creaked and weakened after each onslaught, and then it gave way, ripping from the walls that held it, tearing out and flattening with a crash. Jack hurtled through, stumbling—and felt a sharp pain shoot through the sole of his right foot.

He had stepped on a nail from the battered door, and the nail was sticking through the bottom of his shoe and into his foot.

Instantly he sat down on the floor of the new room. He pulled out the nail, took off the shoe and the sock, turned up the foot, and squeezed. There was blood, but not much. It was not too bad. The nail had pierced the sole of the foot, but not far. There was no time now for first aid.

He picked up the shoe and examined it. There was a clear, round hole through the bottom leather. No time for first aid—but sufficient time to protect the foot from the wetness of the streets and the danger of infection.

Sitting on the floor, he looked about. The room had a long table, and at its side was a wastepaper basket. On one foot and carrying the shoe, Jack hopped to the wastepaper basket, dug in, and grabbed a sheet of paper.

Now he hopped back to his sock, sat again on the floor, and laid down the shoe. He folded the paper, folded it again and again, and placed it against the hole in the shoe. It would be a makeshift inner sole, but it would do. He put on his sock, made sure the square of folded paper inside the shoe covered the hole, and carefully slipped his foot into the shoe.

Now he stood up, flattening his weight against the makeshift inner sole, testing. The pain was minimal. He took a last look about, crossed the room to a door on the far side, and went through.

And so he went through rooms and doors until he was at the last door—and then he was outside in the street glistening with rain. He observed the number of the house—110. He walked quickly to the corner and looked up at the street sign. Fitchburg Lane.

Jack Power walked rapidly in the rain, away from the house that was 110 Fitchburg Lane.

7   *More Telephone Calls*

Chip was awakened by the shrill ring of the telephone. He looked at the clock as he lifted the receiver. It was seven o'clock. "Hello?" he said into the mouthpiece.

"Chip? Jack."

"Hi. What happened to you?"

"Me?" Jack said. "How do you know *anything* happened to me?"

"Dick Donovan called. He said you had disappeared."

"Yeah." Jack's voice sounded tired. "I'll tell you when I see you. Dad home?"

"I'll go see."

"You'll go *see!*" Jack exclaimed.

"I'm in bed. I was taking a nap."

"Okay, go see."

"Hold on."

Chip got out of bed, Blaze happily bouncing after him, and quickly inspected the suite. Then he came back to the phone.

"Nope," he said to Jack. "He's not home yet."

"Good."

"Why 'good'?" Chip asked.

"He didn't have a chance to worry about me." Jack chuckled. Even the chuckle sounded tired.

"You sure you're all right?" Chip asked.

"Just dandy," Jack replied, but he certainly did not sound just dandy. "Look," Jack said, "I should be home in about half an hour or so."

"Where are you?"

"Somewhere uptown. I'm calling from a phone booth. 'Bye, boy. See you later." And, abruptly, Jack hung up.

Chip sighed, replaced the receiver, saw the wallet on the table—and suddenly remembered. He felt guilty. The poor man, whoever he was—Frank Bristol—would have missed it by now and must be terribly worried. Quickly he dialed the number and at once someone answered the phone.

"Yes? Hello?" said a thick, rasping voice.

"Mr. Bristol?"

"Yeah, this is Bristol."

"Did you lose a wallet, sir?"

"What?"

"A wallet. I found—"

"Just a minute."

After a few moments the voice came back on the wire, but it sounded much more pleasant. "Yes, I did lose my wallet—and I didn't even know it."

"I found it, sir."

"I imagine you did, or else you wouldn't be calling about it."

"This afternoon in a drugstore," Chip said. "You were in the phone booth. I rushed out after you, but you were already out of sight."

"I must say, you're a very honest young man."

For a moment Chip wondered how the person on the other end of the wire knew that he, Chip, was a *young* man. Then he realized that his voice, of course, was certainly not that of an *old* man.

"Anyway, it's all safe and sound," Chip declared.

"Thank you so much," Mr. Bristol said. "I'd appreciate if you'd return it right away."

"Right away?" Chip asked somewhat thinly. He was anxious to stay and hear what had happened to Jack.

"It's most important."

"Well . . ." Chip ventured. "I mean—it's already evening. I thought maybe tomorrow, early?"

"Please!" the man begged. "Where are you calling from? Where are you?"

"Thirty-fifth and Lexington."

"Hardly a stone's throw," the man pleaded. "You know the address? It's on the identification card."

"Yes, it is," Chip said.

"Take a cab. I'll reimburse you. It's a short trip. I won't keep you, and you'll be able to get back to whatever you want to do. And there'll be a fine reward for you—which you certainly deserve. Please? Right away? It's *most* important."

The poor man, Chip thought. Of course it was important—all that money!

"All right," Chip said. "But I *do* want to get back as quickly as possible."

"No problem on that score," the man promised.

"Very good, Mr. Bristol. I'm practically on my way right now."

"Thank you very much, young man. Oh—it's apartment twelve-A."

"Yes, sir," Chip said. "See you soon. Good-bye now."

Hurriedly he dressed, took the wallet, patted Blaze, and ran out.

8 *A Ride in the Rain*

Downstairs, it was raining, but as Chip emerged from the hotel, a taxi drew to the curb. The doorman was either sheltering himself from the rain or was busy elsewhere—he was nowhere in sight. The taxi deposited two passengers, a man and a lady, and Chip held the door for them, receiving for his effort their smiles of gratitude. Then he entered the taxi and closed the door.

"Where to, young fella?" the driver said.

"Two-oh-three West Seventy-second Street."

"Yes, sir, young fella," said the driver, making the notation of the address on his trip card. Then he shifted gears and the cab moved forward, the tires making a whining noise on the rain-slick street. "You're my last call," the driver said. "After you, I park the hack in the garage and go home. It's been a long day."

As he had been taught by his father, Chip, sitting forward, made a mental note of the information printed on the driver's cards up front by the dashboard.

The cab number was 33963. The driver's name was Aaron Lindsay.

Chip sighed and sat back and enjoyed the sights as the taxi tooled through the teeming rain. Then suddenly he sat upright, rigid and anxious, beset by problems, many problems.

First, he had forgotten to feed Blaze. The poor dog had not eaten all day.

Next, there was the business of Jack. If Dad came home before Jack, there would be no Jack—and no explanation.

And no Chip, either, for that matter.

And no note, no word, no explanation.

Dad would be frantic!

And right now, this minute, there was an immediate problem—no money! He had no money! How would he pay the taxi fare? But that problem resolved itself quickly. He would pay with Mr. Bristol's money. He would explain that to Mr. Bristol, and of course Mr. Bristol would understand.

So he was back to his other problems.

Should he go back to the hotel, leave a note for Dad, and then start again on the trip to Mr. Bristol?

He looked out the window. They were already on the west side, on Eighth Avenue and 56th Street. That placed them quite near to Mr. Bristol and quite far from the hotel. It would be a pity to go all the way back. . . .

And then he had an idea!

"Mr. Lindsay," he said to the cab driver.

Mr. Lindsay had a hearty, happy voice.

"Yes, young fella, what can I do for you?"

"Please," Chip requested. "If I wrote a note—to

my dad, could you please deliver it back at the hotel where you picked me up—to the desk clerk? I mean, would it be too much trouble?"

"No trouble at all," Mr. Lindsay replied. "After I drop you, I have to go in that direction anyway. It's near where my garage is. Like I told you before, you're my last call. After I drop you, I bring in the cab and I go home."

Chip smiled in relief. "Thank you so much," he said. "And whatever the extra charge is, I'll pay for it."

Mr. Lindsay laughed. "No extra charge, young fella. I'm happy to do you the favor." And then he asked, "Do you have pencil and paper?"

Of course, Chip did *not* have pencil and paper.

"I'm afraid not," Chip murmured.

"I didn't think you did." Mr. Lindsay laughed again as he slid the cab to the curb and put on the brake. He handed back a pencil and a small note pad. "Now, you write your note while we're standing still," he suggested. "And then off we go again."

"Thank you. You're very kind."

"My pleasure, young fella."

Chip wrote:

Dear Dad,

I forgot to feed Blaze. Please feed him. Jack called. He's on his way home. I found a man's wallet and I'm returning it to him. I will share the reward with you (ha ha). See you later.

Chip

He gave note, pad, and pencil to Mr. Lindsay.

"My father's name is Thomas Power. Just leave it with the desk clerk—for Mr. Power."

"Thomas Power," Mr. Lindsay repeated. "Yes, sir, young fella. Consider it as good as done." The cab started up.

Chip was relaxed now. He sat back and looked out the window, watching all the many blurry-yellow lights smeared with rain. And then the taxi stopped.

"Here we are," Mr. Lindsay said. "Two-oh-three West Seventy-second."

The meter showed a charge of $1.80. Chip decided on a fat tip for the kind and obliging Mr. Lindsay. He drew a twenty-dollar bill out of the wallet and handed it forward.

"Please take three dollars out of this," Chip said.

"Well, thank you, young fella." Mr. Lindsay looked at the bill and whistled. "Twenty bucks! My only one today. We don't get many twenties in this business."

He returned seventeen dollars to Chip, who carefully placed the money into the wallet.

Then he got out, waved to Mr. Lindsay, received a wave in return—and the cab sped away.

9 *The Man in Apartment 12-A*

The building at 203 West 72nd Street was tall and old. A flimsy canopy protected Chip from the rain as he read the raised bronze letters of a plaque affixed to the stone wall: CROWLEY ARMS — FURNISHED APARTMENTS.

Inside, there was a small, square vestibule with two closed glass doors. To the right, on the wall, were the name-bells, and alongside each name was the apartment number. Chip pressed the button next to BRISTOL, 12-A. The response was a clicking between the doors, and he pushed through into the lobby.

The lobby was long, narrow, and empty. At the far end were two self-service elevators, both open. Chip entered one, touched the button for the twelfth floor, and the elevator climbed up squeakily.

Apartment 12-A was the first apartment to the left of the elevator. It had no bell. Chip knocked with his knuckles, and the door was opened by the man he remembered from the phone booth in the drugstore on Madison Avenue—dark, flat-nosed, with bushy eyebrows. The man wore his shirt open at the neck.

"Mr. Bristol?" Chip inquired.

"Yeah. I'm Bristol."

"Chip Power."

"Who?" The bushy eyebrows frowned over deep-set, tiny black eyes.

"I—I found your wallet . . ." Chip began.

"Oh, yes!" The rasping voice became more pleasant. "Come right in."

The living room was small, airless, and messy. There were clothes strewn all over the place. The burly man took his jacket off an easy chair, tossed it to another chair, and motioned Chip to the easy chair. Chip sat and the dust from the chair rose up around him.

"Do you have it?" Mr. Bristol asked.

"Oh, sure." Chip took the wallet from his pocket.

Bristol snatched it from Chip's hand and laid it on a table.

Then lamely, almost as an afterthought, he said, "Thank you."

"Don't mention it," Chip replied. He smiled. "You know, Mr. Bristol, there's something I don't understand."

"Don't understand what?" Bristol asked.

"Well, on the phone you said that you didn't know that you'd lost your wallet. I mean—a *wallet!*"

Bristol laughed. He had yellowish teeth. He put a meaty hand into a side pocket of his trousers and pulled out a wad of bills.

"Y'see," he said, "actually I keep my money in my pants' pocket, so I hardly ever use the wallet. So

I didn't even know I lost it."

"But that wallet's *full* of money," Chip exclaimed. "All those twenty-dollar bills!"

"Well, that's kind of special money," Bristol rumbled. "I was bringing it to the bank, to my vault. But I got busy today—so I was going to bring it tomorrow morning. Then, like a dope, I go and lose it."

"Well," Chip commented. "A thing like that can happen to anybody."

"I'll show you how it happened," Bristol said and turned around, his free hand touching the flap of a rear pocket. "There's supposed to be a button here, see? Well, the button fell off, and I didn't know it. And that's where I keep the wallet, in this back pocket. Understand what happened?"

"Yes, I think so," Chip said.

"What happened," Bristol explained, "was, while I was sitting in the phone booth, the wallet edges up and there's no button-down flap to hold it. So it's all the way up and loose, like that. Then when I

stand up and go, it just falls out. Pretty stupid of me, hey?"

"No, sir, I wouldn't say that," Chip replied crisply. "Just an unfortunate accident, the button falling off and all."

"Well, it's a good thing a fine, honest boy found it," Bristol declared. "And now like I promised—a reward." He peeled off two bills from the wad in his hand. "Let's say ten dollars for the reward—and an extra five to pay you for taking a taxi up and back. Okay, kid?"

"Oh, no," Chip said.

Bristol looked confused.

"What's the matter? Not enough?" he rasped.

"Gee, no. It—it seems like too much," Chip said.

Bristol blinked his beady black eyes. "I don't get you, kid. I don't understand."

"Well, you see, sir," Chip explained, "there's no need for you to reimburse me for my trip up here."

"But I did promise you—"

"I didn't have the money to pay the taxi driver,"

Chip continued, "so I paid him with one of your twenty-dollar bills. I gave him a big tip, too, because he was very kind. Three dollars. So if you will please deduct three dollars—"

"You paid him with one of my twenty-dollar bills?" Bristol thundered.

"But—but what's the difference?" Chip stammered. "I mean, what's the difference if I pay with your money in advance, or if you return the money to me afterward?"

"Yeah, no difference," Bristol grumbled.

But Chip could see the man was very disturbed. Bristol's face had become red as a berry, and the muscles at the points of his jaw were quivering.

"Gee, I hope I didn't do anything wrong," Chip remarked anxiously.

"You're a fine, honest boy," Bristol muttered. "You could have taken advantage of me, but you didn't. Just for that, I have an even better reward for you."

Bristol strode on sturdy legs to a desk drawer and

came back with a gleaming golden pen.

"Gee, that's beautiful," Chip said admiringly.

"It's for you," Bristol said, holding it at Chip's face.

"Please, no," Chip protested. "I can't accept a gift as expensive as that. I mean, after all, all I did was return a wallet."

He would have liked to examine the beautiful golden pen, but it was out of focus, Bristol shoving it closer and closer under his nose.

Then Bristol pressed the clasp of the pen.

Chip heard the hiss of the escaping gas and fell back in the dusty chair, unconscious.

10 *Explanations*

At the desk of the Hotel Lincoln, Mr. Thomas Power received Chip's note, which the desk clerk had kindly enclosed in an envelope. There was also a message from Mr. Barry Donovan—would Mr. Power please call Mr. Donovan at his home?

Upstairs in suite 903 Mr. Power was greeted by a boisterous Blaze, who temporarily forgot his hunger in the delight at seeing his master.

Mr. Power patted Blaze, slit open the envelope, read Chip's note, shook his head, and smiled. Then immediately he took Blaze to the kitchen and fed him.

And now in the living room, at the telephone, he was about to call Mr. Donovan when he heard the key scrape in the lock—and Jack entered.

"Jack!" Mr. Power cried, hurrying to him.

Jack looked dreadful. His face was pale, his eyes were haggard, and his clothes were damp and wrinkled.

"Jack! What is it? What's the matter?"

Jack tried for a smile but only succeeded in looking more ill. "I'm—I'm okay, Dad."

"All right," Mr. Power commanded. "Before you do a thing, before you say a word—get out of those wet clothes. Wash up, have a glass of hot milk or something, and put on some dry things. Then come back here and tell me what this is all about."

Jack went to the bedroom, removed his clothes, and put his shoes in the closet. Then he had a hot shower and treated his foot. He cleansed the wound, which was quite tiny, put on antiseptic, and covered it with an adhesive strip. He dressed again in slacks, white wool socks, loafers, and a sport shirt. He combed his hair, observing himself in the mirror. He did not feel much better, but he did look much better. He went to the living room and there found Mr. Power pacing worriedly.

"Please, Dad, I'm all right," he said.

"Now, what is this all about?" Mr. Power demanded.

In as few words as possible, Jack tiredly stated the facts as best he could, at that moment, remember them.

"Unbelievable!" Mr. Power cried. "Of all things —a kidnapping!"

Jack grinned wanly. "But who would want to kidnap *me?*"

"That's not for me—or you—to try to answer," Mr. Power declared. "This is a police matter."

He went to the phone and called his friend, Detective James Wilson. He began to tell the story, but Detective Wilson interrupted.

"Just stay put," Detective Wilson said. "I'll be over as fast as I can get there. I think I ought to hear this whole story directly from Jack."

"Thank you, Jim."

"Not at all, Tom. Keep the boy resting. I'll see you in a few minutes."

They said good-bye and Mr. Power hung up.

"Detective Wilson is on his way," Mr. Power said to Jack. "I could tell from his tone how disturbed he is." Mr. Power sighed. "After all, he has known you since you were practically a baby."

"He's been almost like a second father to me," Jack said.

"Well, you just lie down there on the couch and rest. Oh! Here's a note from Chip."

While Jack was stretched on the couch reading Chip's note, Mr. Power returned Mr. Donovan's call.

"How did it go at the airport?" Mr. Donovan inquired.

"Very well, sir," Mr. Power replied.

"Actually, Thomas, that's not why I called you. When Dick came home from the ball game, he told me—well, a sort of peculiar story about your Jack. Frankly, I was a bit worried. Is he all right?"

"He's all right—now."

"I don't understand, Thomas."

Mr. Power quickly recited the events.

"Good grief!" Mr. Donovan cried. "Absolutely dreadful! He's quite a lad to have gotten out of it as he did. You say the police are on their way?"

"Yes, they're on their way right now, Mr. Donovan."

"Well, do please keep me informed, Thomas."

"Of course I shall, Mr. Donovan. Thank you so much for calling."

Mr. Power hung up. Jack got off the couch and returned Chip's note to his father.

"Leave it to Chip," Jack said. "Always something."

"*Always* something—one or the other of you," Mr. Power said crossly. Then a look of concern came over his face and he said quite tenderly, "Hungry, Son? I'll prepare a bite for you."

"Thanks, Dad, no."

"But you haven't eaten all day."

"Maybe later. You know how it is."

"Yes, I sure do."

Nevertheless, Mr. Power went to the kitchen and came back with a small sandwich and a glass of milk.

Dutifully, but without appetite, Jack ate, and he was grateful. He *did* feel somewhat better after eating something.

There was a knock, and Mr. Power opened the door for Detective James Wilson and two other men in plain clothes. Detective Wilson introduced them as technical men, fingerprint experts.

"And now, if you please," Detective Wilson said to Jack, "let's have your tale of woe, young man."

"It'll be a little mixed up," Jack confessed. "I still can't get it all straight in my own mind."

"Naturally not, after all you've been through." Detective Wilson took out a small notebook and a pen. "You just tell it to me as best you can."

Jack told his story. As Jack talked, Detective Wilson took notes.

"I've probably left out a few things," Jack said.

"Probably, but in time they'll all come back to you. Under the circumstances, you've done very well indeed." Detective Wilson smiled. He was a tall man with white hair and keen gray eyes. "Now, Jack, I'm going to ask you some important questions."

"Shoot," Jack said, smiling.

"I'd like a description of the man who actually did the kidnapping."

Jack closed his eyes and frowned. "Medium height. Stocky. Black hair. Black eyes. Kind of bushy eyebrows. A flat nose—as if it had been broken long ago in a fight." Jack opened his eyes. "And he has a kind of thick voice. You know, a kind of rasping voice."

"Excellent," Detective Wilson said, taking notes. "Would you recognize him if you saw him again?"

"Oh, no question," Jack declared. "Absolutely."

"Good boy. And now about the other one—the one with the vaguely familiar voice." Detective Wilson fixed his gray eyes firmly upon Jack. "How do you mean that—familiar?"

Rather lamely, Jack had to admit, "I—I really don't know."

"Do you mean that you've heard it before?"

"I—I really can't say." Jack shrugged.

"Perhaps familiar," Detective Wilson coaxed, "because it sounds similar to somebody *else's* voice. Perhaps a voice that is similar to that of somebody you know?"

"I—I wish I could tell you," Jack said.

"Easy does it, lad." Detective Wilson smiled understandingly. "After this excitement dies down, and after you've had some rest, it's very likely it will come back to you, clear and sharp."

"I hope so," Jack said.

There was a silence while Detective Wilson consulted his notes.

"Now, let's see," he reviewed. "The rasping

voice and the vaguely familiar voice—those two went away. Correct?"

"Yes."

"Leaving you with the third man."

"Yes, correct," Jack said.

"Now what about him? Any ideas?"

Jack shook his head. "Not one idea at all."

"Now, don't sound so sad about it, Jack." Detective Wilson laughed. "You're doing very well. Very well indeed."

"This is doing very well?" Jack asked with a wry grin.

"As a matter of fact, I wish to compliment you. Besides your courage and your skill in breaking out of there, you had the presence of mind to note the address."

"One-ten Fitchburg Lane," Jack murmured.

Detective Wilson looked toward Mr. Power. "That's quite a distance from here—up in the Bronx." He put away his notebook and pen. "I suggest we go up there. Now! I realize it's tough on poor Jack here, but it's necessary."

"Oh, I'm perfectly willing," Jack said.

"Do you need me?" Mr. Power inquired of Detective Wilson.

"No." Detective Wilson looked perplexed. "But I'd imagine you'd *want* to go, Tom."

"I certainly do," Mr. Power declared and sighed. "But I have two sons, as you know, Jim, and the other one's off on some crazy adventure of his own. I believe I ought to be here when he gets back."

"I'm with you, Dad," Jack agreed.

"In that case, let's go," Detective Wilson said. "I'll have Jack back here in short order, Tom." He laughed. "In a police car—coming or going—you can travel pretty fast."

11   *"The House on Fitchburg Lane"*

The rain had finally ceased. The summer storm was over. Stars were beginning to sparkle in the evening sky.

Jack sat in the rear with Detective Wilson as the police car, top light flashing and siren wailing, sped north to the Bronx. The streets whizzed by, and then the city was left behind and they were in a rather rugged area—trees, marshes, vacant lots stuffed with tall weeds, unpaved roads, and not too many houses.

Soon the car stopped at 110 Fitchburg Lane.

"Is this it?" asked Detective Wilson.

"This is it," Jack replied.

They got out, all four of them. Jack looked about. Now he had time for inspection.

The house stood alone, dark. It was surrounded by wild vegetation—matted shrubs, crabgrass, stumpy little trees. There was no house near.

Detective Wilson glanced at the two plainclothesmen. He made no signal, but they understood. They drew pistols from holsters hidden beneath their jackets.

Jack's heart beat wildly as he and Detective Wilson followed behind them. All four advanced upon the entrance—and stopped. Carefully one of the plainclothesmen tried the knob. The door was unlocked. He pushed, and the door creaked open into darkness.

Silence. Darkness and silence.

Pushing Jack behind him, Detective Wilson moved forward. He reached into his clothes and brought forth a searchlight.

"Cover me," he whispered to his men.

Boldly he stepped into the darkness, the beam of his searchlight playing before him. On either side of him a pistol was held in readiness for whoever might be lurking within.

The white beam of light roved about the room.

Nothing! No sound. No living being.

"Hello!" Detective Wilson called.

There was no answer, except his own echo.

The beam found a switch. Detective Wilson clicked it.

They were in a poorly-furnished living room.

"Hello!" Detective Wilson called again.

Again his only response was the echo of his own voice.

"The way I figure it, our birds have flown," one of the detectives said.

"I agree," Detective Wilson conceded. "Once they learned of the boy's escape, they quickly made certain of their own escape. Let's have a look, eh? But let's not let our guard down."

They went from room to room, clicking on the

lights. The house was empty. They saw the room where Jack had been held prisoner. They saw the battered door. They saw the wastepaper basket, but it was empty. They could not find a single thing that was of any use to them, and then they discovered why.

In the yard in the rear of the house was an incinerator. It was still smoking. All scraps of paper, everything, had been thoroughly burned. Detective Wilson sighed.

"So much for any incriminating evidence," he said solemnly. "However, there's still work to do."

The two plainclothesmen set about dusting the rooms for fingerprints. Jack remained with Detective Wilson.

Detective Wilson called the Bronx police, inquiring about the ownership of the house at 110 Fitchburg Lane. He learned that the house was owned by a Mrs. Maggi Burns, a widow, who lived at 52 Putnam Street, which was about a mile from the house on Fitchburg Lane.

"Do you want to go?" he asked Jack.

"I'd love it," Jack answered.

They left the two detectives busily working and swiftly drove the mile to Putnam Street. Mrs. Burns lived in an attractive little white house with a red roof and well-tended lawn. Detective Wilson rang the bell, showed his credentials to Mrs. Maggi Burns, and they were admitted to a clean and well-kept parlor. Quickly and urgently Detective Wilson explained the reason for their visit.

"Oh, my!" exclaimed Mrs. Burns. Then she added, smiling sweetly, "You're the first detective I've ever met in all my life!"

She was tiny and very old, but she had rosy cheeks and lively blue eyes that sparkled like sunshine on water. She invited them to sit down, which they did, and then offered refreshments, which they declined.

"And now, about the house on Fitchburg Lane . . ." Detective Wilson began.

"It was left to me by my late husband," Mrs. Burns declared. "It is—what is the expression?—a white

elephant. It's in a rather bad neighborhood, you know. I have tried to sell it, but without success, so I have been renting it."

Detective Wilson perked up.

"Could you tell me to whom you last rented it?" he inquired.

"A man by the name of Frank Smith."

"Frank Smith," Detective Wilson repeated. "And when was this?"

"About a month ago," Mrs. Burns replied. "The rental is seventy-five dollars a month. Mr. Smith paid six months in advance."

"Six months in advance! But why?"

"Well, Mr. Smith said that he was a writer working on a book—that he wanted to be alone, that he did not want to be disturbed. This was quite all right with me." Mrs. Burns smiled. "I have no desire to go into that neighborhood, even to collect rent."

"I see," Detective Wilson said. "And what references did he give you?"

"Frankly, I didn't ask for any." The old lady

laughed a tinkling little laugh which did not quite hide her embarrassment. "You see, I was so happy to get rid of my—my white elephant—for six months, I just didn't want to ask too many questions. He paid me for the full six months, in cash, in advance. I—I just didn't want to spoil it with too many questions. He seemed a nice enough man, and I had nothing to lose. There's absolutely nothing of any value in that house that anybody would want to steal."

Detective Wilson sighed and stood up, and Jack followed suit.

"By the way, what did this Frank Smith look like?" Detective Wilson asked.

"Oh, a nice enough man," Mrs. Burns replied lightly. "Dark eyes, dark hair. He was very polite indeed."

"Any distinguishing feature?" Detective Wilson inquired.

Mrs. Burns knitted her brows.

"Yes," she said finally. "His nose. It was sort of

flat—sort of broken, you know? It gave him a kind of fierce look. But I couldn't hold *that* against the poor man, now, could I?"

"Of course not," Detective Wilson answered rather glumly. "Well, thank you very much, Mrs. Burns," he said. "Sorry to have troubled you."

"Oh, no trouble at all, sir."

In the car going back to the house on Fitchburg Lane, Detective Wilson grumbled, "Frank Smith. Obviously, of course, a phony name, an alias. But we can't blame that sweet old lady, can we?"

Jack made no reply, and so they lapsed into silence.

Back at 110 Fitchburg Lane the news was all bad.

"Nothing," one of the detectives declared. "They were careful. No fingerprints. The only ones we got we found in the room where the kid was kept prisoner, and those are probably his."

They tested the tips of Jack's fingers, and that was

the end of the investigation in the Bronx. The sum total had produced only Jack Power's fingerprints. They drove back toward the city in a discouraged silence, broken only once by a conversation between Detective Wilson and Jack.

"There's one last hope," Detective Wilson muttered.

"What?" Jack asked.

"I'll take you down to headquarters and have you look at pictures in the rogues' gallery. Maybe you'll turn up Flatnose for us. You've had a rough day, I know, but this is the one last thing I'll ask of you. Are you up to it?"

Gamely Jack said, "Sure."

"We'll drop in on your dad first."

"Sure," Jack said.

But in suite 903 of the Hotel Lincoln they found Thomas Power pacing worriedly.

"No sign of Chip—no word, nothing," he said. Mr. Power's face was deeply lined with anxiety.

"What's *this* all about?" Detective Wilson demanded.

Mr. Power showed him Chip's note.

"How long has he been gone?"

"I talked to him on the phone at about seven o'clock this evening," Jack said.

Detective Wilson tried to sound cheerful, but his face looked grave.

"You know how it is with youngsters," he said to Mr. Power. "He's probably enjoying his adventure and has forgotten about the time."

"Not Chip," Mr. Power responded. "He's not stupid. He'd know that by now I'd be terribly worried."

"Well, Chip *can* be flighty," Jack said, trying to comfort his father. But he himself, despite his own fatigue, looked worried.

"Let's just give it a little more time," Detective Wilson interposed. "I'm taking Jack down for a look-see at the rogues' gallery." He gave Mr. Power a quick recital of what they had accomplished—or, actually, what they had *not* accomplished—in the Bronx. "Let's give Chip just that much more time. Okay?"

Mr. Power nodded. "All right. I'll stay here, of course."

The rogues' gallery produced no face that Jack Power recognized, so Detective Wilson drove him back to the hotel. It was quite late now.

"No success downtown," Detective Wilson informed Mr. Power.

"Jim, I really don't care about that at this moment," Mr. Power cried. "We *do* have Jack safe and sound. But where in the world is Chip?"

Detective Wilson tried, but failed, to cover up his expression of concern.

"Tom, I'm sure he's all right. You know how kids are." But despite his bright words of encouragement, he went slowly to the telephone. "Just as a matter of routine," he said, "I'll phone downtown and report him as a missing person."

Mr. Power made no response. He continued

pacing and wringing his hands.

Jack slumped into an easy chair, fighting fatigue, trying to stay alert.

Detective Wilson talked into the telephone, telling about Chip, giving a description of the boy whom he knew so well. ". . . and if you hear anything, anything at all," he added, "call me directly at my home, and don't worry about waking me whatever time it may be."

Detective Wilson hung up.

"Tom," he said, "please try not to worry. There's no word of any accident, nothing like that. He'll be all right, you'll see. Any report during the night and I'll be in touch with you."

"What could have happened to him?" Jack cried.

"Try to get some sleep," Detective Wilson said soothingly. "Both of you. The gears are in mesh; the police department is working on it. They'll turn him up for you, believe me. If it happens during the night, I'll call you. If not, I'll be here early tomorrow morning. Now, do try to get some rest, both of you."

12   *"The Waiting Game"*

At that very moment, Chip Power, after a long, deep sleep, opened his eyes.

He was lying on his back on the concrete floor of a damp, stone-walled basement. His wrists and ankles were tied and his mouth was gagged.

He could see, high above him, through small, barred windows, a pale silver moon and summer stars.

He felt groggy and dizzy from the gas that had made him unconscious.

For a few minutes he had no recollection of what had happened to him. He closed his eyes and lay breathing deeply as memory slowly returned. Then, flooded by recollection, he opened his eyes and looked about, remembering all.

He was in a bare, stone room, a cellar. To his left there was a long, steep flight of wooden stairs topped by a sturdy, closed door. There were three high, small, barred windows, through which, like slim silver rivers, pale shafts of moonlight poured in upon him.

There was nothing in the room; it was entirely empty. The floor was of concrete and the walls were of stone, but the high ceiling was of ordinary plaster; it was old and rotten.

There was a large crumbling hole in the plaster. Through the hole Chip could see spaced strips of wood, the rotting slats beyond the plaster of the ceiling.

One of the high, barred windows was open for air, and a smell came through—a fresh, salt smell. And there was a sound, a constant sound, a faint swishing noise from outside which Chip could not quite make out. He shook his aching head.

And then came a sound which he *could* make out
—the ringing of a telephone. He heard it clearly
through the rotting slats of the hole in the ceiling.
And he heard the rasping voice of Frank Bristol
talking on the telephone:

"Yes, this is Frank. . . . I've checked out of there
for good. . . . Yes, I'll be right here by the long
beach house. I'll be staying here for good. . . . Sure
we've got to get rid of him, but not here, not near
this house—far away from here. . . . Okay, tomorrow morning. We'll do it together, you and me. . . .
Okay, I'll see you in the morning."

Frank Bristol hung up. Chip heard his footsteps
receding, going to another part of the house.

Now he lay quietly, thinking. Now he understood
the faint swishing sounds from outside. They were
waves from the sea, lapping at the shore, swishing
on the sand. He had learned much from Frank Bristol's conversation: that he was in a beach house, that
it was a long house, that Bristol would be remaining

here for good. And he had learned more: that they intended to do him harm, *that they were going to get rid of him!* But not tonight! Tomorrow morning!

Why? He wondered. What had he done to make this man his enemy? Why would Frank Bristol want to harm him?

He thought back to the conversation in apartment 12-A at 203 West 72nd Street. It had been perfectly innocent. He had returned the man's wallet. They had gotten along very pleasantly until he had told Mr. Bristol that he had used one of the twenty-dollar bills to pay the taxi driver. Right then Mr. Bristol had become angry. But being angry is one thing. Kidnapping is another.

Why? *What had he done that could be so terrible?*

Chip struggled with that but could find no explanation. Now he turned his mind to what had actually happened. He tried to reconstruct the events.

The pen! The golden pen!

It contained some kind of gas, a sleeping gas. Press a certain part of the pen, and the gas escaped. Bristol had shoved it under his nose. He remembered the hiss. He had inhaled the gas and had become unconscious.

Then what?

Bristol had taken him down in the elevator, holding him as though he were a sick boy. Chip could imagine it exactly. Bristol had then half-dragged, half-led him into a car, and driven him out to this place. Then he had tied him up and put him into this stone basement room.

Chip tested his bonds. Not too bad. He was not tied too well. Of course not. Bristol had not bothered. What could Chip do even if he untied himself? He was still locked inside the stone room. Of course the door was locked. Untied, what could he do? The windows were high up. There was nothing in sight, no ladder that could help him reach them. And even if he did, they had bars on them. The door? It was at the head of the steep stairway.

There was no space for a run so that he could hurl himself at the door. And even if the door was on a flat surface—the first sound of trying to break out would immediately alert his captor.

For a few moments, nevertheless, Chip thought about that. He thought about untying himself, banging at the door, and taking his chances with Frank Bristol. He thought about it—and rejected it. The man was far too powerful. In a fight, Bristol would win hands down.

No. In a contest of strength, he would lose. He would have to use his brains. He would have to figure the angles. He would have to play the waiting game—watch and wait, and grasp an opportunity if and when it presented itself. But he *would* have to be prepared!

Preparation! The first thing to do was to loosen his bonds. He had all night.

Wriggling his wrists, fingers, ankles, toes, all the muscles of his body, Chip Power concentrated upon the cords that restrained him.

13 *The Missing Link*

Jack Power slept the sleep of the just, but Mr. Thomas Power turned and twisted all night. By eight o'clock he had already had breakfast, and at nine he made breakfast for Jack, and at nine-thirty he could no longer wait and called Detective Wilson.

"I was just about to come over," Detective Wilson said. "I'll be there in ten minutes."

"Any news?"

"Nothing."

Detective Wilson arrived at a quarter to ten. He knocked and Jack opened the door for him.

"Hi," Jack greeted him.

"Hi," Detective Wilson responded. Then, turning to Mr. Power, he said, "How are you, Tom?"

"Just worried to death," Mr. Power replied.

"Easy does it, my friend. Patience." Detective Wilson tried to sound cheerful, but Jack could see that he was as worried as Mr. Power. "In a case like this," Detective Wilson added, "no news is good news."

"Now, what does that mean?" Mr. Power inquired wearily.

"It means that if anything had happened to young Chip—any accident or any harm—there would have been some report on it. There has been none—no report to any precinct all during the night. I know it's small comfort, Tom, but it *is* a comfort."

They were startled by a sudden, sharp rapping on the door.

"That might be Chip!" Jack shouted and rushed to open the door.

It was not Chip.

Two men stood in the doorway. One was tall and lean. The other was short and chubby. Detective Wilson recognized the tall man at once.

"Lieutenant Cassidy!" Detective Wilson declared pleasantly, but his frown was one of amazement. "What are *you* doing here?"

"I might ask the same question," retorted Detective Wilson's fellow officer.

The short, chubby man coughed impatiently.

"Oh," Lieutenant Cassidy said. "This gentleman is Aaron Lindsay. He's a taxi driver."

"Look. Please," Mr. Power interposed. "Does this have anything to do with my son?"

"I should say it does," asserted Mr. Lindsay.

"Where is he?" demanded Mr. Power.

"Where *is* he?" Mr. Lindsay repeated and looked astonished.

Lieutenant Cassidy raised his hands. "Now, just hold it, please, everybody!"

They were all silent.

"Yesterday evening," Lieutenant Cassidy explained, "this man, Mr. Aaron Lindsay, drove your son in his taxi—"

"How does he know it was my son?" Mr. Power interjected.

"The boy wrote a note," Lieutenant Cassidy replied. "He asked Mr. Lindsay to deliver it here to the desk clerk. It was a note to his father—Mr. Thomas Power. We're quite anxious to talk to that young man."

"So are we," Detective Wilson declared.

"What do you mean?" exclaimed Lieutenant Cassidy.

Detective Wilson was quivering with excitement. Here, at last, was the first clue in the disappearance of Chip Power. Quickly he explained the situation to Lieutenant Cassidy and then took over the interrogation of Aaron Lindsay.

"You drove this boy in your taxi?"

"Yes, sir."

"Where did you pick him up?"

"Right here outside the hotel."

"When was this?"

"Yesterday evening." Mr. Lindsay took out his trip card from an inside pocket, unfolded it, and looked at it. "It was a quarter after seven yesterday evening. He was my last call."

"Where did you take him?" Detective Wilson demanded. "Did you mark down the address on your trip card?" He held his breath, hoping, praying.

"Of course," replied Mr. Lindsay, and then he read from the trip card, "Two-oh-three West Seventy-second Street."

Detective Wilson paced excitedly. Now they were getting somewhere!

He returned to the taxi driver. "Mr. Lindsay, will you please explain to me why, exactly, you are here now?"

"If you'll only give me a chance. . . ."

Detective Wilson smiled broadly. "I'm sorry. All yours now. Go right ahead."

"Well," Mr. Lindsay sighed, "it was like this. I

drove him up there and promised to deliver the note back here. Like I said, he was my last call. He paid me with a twenty-dollar bill—"

Now it was Mr. Power who interrupted. "A twenty-dollar bill! Chip didn't have a twenty-dollar bill!"

Mr. Lindsay sighed again, then shrugged. "All I know is that the boy pays me with a twenty-dollar bill. It's the only twenty-dollar bill I took in. This morning I go to the bank to make a deposit. They tell me the twenty-dollar bill is a phony, a counterfeit. They call in cops—this man, Lieutenant Cassidy. I tell him the whole story—and that's why we're here."

"All quite true," Lieutenant Cassidy agreed. "Here, take a look at it, Jim."

He took a bill from his pocket and showed it to Detective Wilson.

Detective Wilson examined it closely.

"A pretty bad counterfeit," he stated as he returned it to Lieutenant Cassidy.

"Bad." Lieutenant Cassidy nodded. "The teller at the bank spotted it immediately."

"Jack, please," Detective Wilson called. "May I have Chip's note?"

Jack brought out the note. Detective Wilson displayed it to Lieutenant Cassidy.

"Beginning to come clear?" Detective Wilson asked.

"Sure is," Lieutenant Cassidy replied slowly. "Mr. Power says the boy didn't have a twenty-dollar bill—"

"Matter of fact, I'm certain he was *short* of money," Mr. Power declared. "I had to go off on business. . . ."

"The note says he found a man's wallet and was returning it," Lieutenant Cassidy continued. "Since he was short of money, he naturally paid with money from the wallet, planning to explain it to the owner when he saw him."

"And if the owner knew it was a counterfeit bill," Detective Wilson said, "then he also knew he was in trouble. The one person who could incriminate him, then, was Chip Power. So now we have a good and sufficient reason why Chip Power is missing."

"No!" Mr. Power groaned.

In terror Jack whispered, "They might kill him."

Detective Wilson was pale and his expression was very grave.

"I think we'd all better get up there to two-oh-three West Seventy-second Street. Right now."

Outside, it was a hot and sunny morning. They sped through the streets in two cars, Wilson's and Cassidy's, and at the Crowley Arms they went immediately to the superintendent.

There they learned that one person had checked out yesterday—Frank Bristol, of apartment 12-A.

"Mr. Bristol called late last night," the superintendent said.

"He said he was checking out for good. No trouble on that score. The tenants pay by the week, in advance."

"What did this Bristol look like?" Detective Wilson queried.

"A husky man," the superintendent replied. "Dark, heavy black eyebrows, a kind of busted nose."

Jack and Detective Wilson exchanged glances.

"Could be one and the same guy," Detective Wilson said.

"Sure," Jack agreed. "After all, Chip was with me at Mr. Donovan's house. Flatnose was outside there in the neighborhood. Chip found his wallet—"

"Take us up to twelve-A, please," Detective Wilson said to the superintendent.

They were certain that Frank Bristol was their man, but they took no chances. Lieutenant Cassidy called for reinforcements, and every occupant's apartment was checked and cleared. There was no question but that Frank Bristol, missing, and Chip Power, missing, were linked together. Detective Wilson called down to headquarters for any information on Frank Bristol. There was no record of arrest.

"Look, there's no use your wasting time here,"

Lieutenant Cassidy said to Wilson. "The counterfeit angle—that's my job. The missing person—that's your job. I'll go over this apartment with a fine-tooth comb, my technical experts and myself. Anything we learn, I'll be in touch with you."

"Excellent."

Detective Wilson shook hands with Lieutenant Cassidy, and he and Mr. Power and Jack returned to the hotel. As they entered the lobby, the desk clerk called to Mr. Power.

"I have a message for you from a Mr. Barry Donovan," the desk clerk said and handed across a folded slip of paper.

Mr. Power opened it and read:

About Jack's disappearance yesterday—please come to my home at once when you receive this. Urgent!

14   *"Mistaken Identity"*

Mrs. Sylvia Donovan herself opened the door for them. She led Mr. Power, Detective Wilson, and Jack to the living room. Dick Donovan was there with his father. Mr. Donovan's round face was beet-red and his blue eyes were hard as marbles, glinting with suppressed anger. Everybody shook hands, and Mr. Power introduced Detective Wilson.

"Detective?" inquired Mr. Donovan.

"New York City Police Department," Wilson informed him.

"Mr. Wilson is an old and dear friend of mine," Mr. Power said.

"Good, good," nodded Mr. Donovan. "I did not want to call the police until after I'd talked with you, Thomas. Now, well—we have the police right here with us. Very good."

"What's it all about?" Detective Wilson asked softly.

"Please get that letter, Dick," Mr. Donovan said to his son.

Dick brought a letter from the mantelpiece and handed it to Detective Wilson. The envelope was addressed by means of letters and numbers cut out from a newspaper and pasted on. Detective Wilson squinted, then withdrew the letter. It was a single sheet of cheap paper with pasted-on newspaper print. It read:

> If you want your son back, prepare $50,000 in unmarked bills. If you call in the police, you will never see your son alive. We will be in touch with you.

Detective Wilson passed it along to Mr. Power, who read it and passed it along to Jack. Jack read it and gave it to Dick Donovan, who returned it to the mantelpiece.

"Do you understand now?" Mr. Donovan asked Mr. Power.

"I believe I do," Mr. Power replied.

"Mistaken identity," Mr. Donovan snapped. "These boys do look very much alike—Jack and Dick. They abducted the wrong one."

"Sure, that's it," Jack cried. "You went up for the binoculars, Dick. I was out there alone, and the guy thought that *I* was Dick Donovan!"

"Exactly," Mr. Donovan thundered. "So you see, gentlemen, this is my problem entirely, and I'm going to see it through to the finish!" He turned to Detective Wilson. "And now, please, what steps do I take?"

Detective Wilson smiled. "You already have."

"Don't I have to call in a formal complaint?"

"No, sir. I'll take care of everything."

"One thing," Mr. Donovan admonished. "I don't want to be swamped with newspaper people. I'd

like this to be handled as privately as possible. I certainly wouldn't enjoy this kind of publicity for myself and my family."

"I'll do my best," Detective Wilson promised.

"Thank you," said Mr. Donovan. "Just one more item, and then it's all yours, Detective Wilson."

"Yes?" inquired Detective Wilson.

"A reward," Mr. Donovan declared. "I hereby offer a reward of five thousand dollars to any person who effects the arrest of the kidnapper. You may inform your colleagues, Detective Wilson, and whomever else you please of the offer of this reward. Five thousand dollars for the arrest of the person who attempted to abduct my son and took young Jack Power by mistake. Thank God he's safe; thank God they're both safe. And now, gentlemen, a bit of lunch."

Mr. Power declined, but Mr. and Mrs. Donovan insisted they all stay for lunch. Mr. Power called the hotel to inquire if, possibly, Chip had come home. He had not. Mr. Power gave the desk clerk

Mr. Donovan's phone number.

"If my younger son comes in or telephones," Mr. Power instructed the desk clerk, "please call me and tell me."

"Yes, sir, I'll do that immediately if he comes in."

"Thank you." Mr. Power hung up.

Barry Donovan wrinkled the corners of his eyes in a frown.

"Now, what's this all about, Thomas?"

And so, to the bewildered Donovans, Mr. Power related all he knew about the disappearance of Chip Power.

15   *"Call the Police!"*

And now, with the sun brilliantly streaming in through the high barred windows, Chip heard the voices through the hole in the ceiling.

Bristol said, "It's about time you showed up."

The other voice said, "I got held up in the traffic."

"Okay, now you're here," Bristol rasped. "Let's take care of the kid."

"How?"

"We'll get him out of here. A long way. Far away from this house."

"Where?" the strange voice asked.

"We'll take him up to Montauk, and we'll get rid

of him there," Bristol retorted. "You go outside and wait in the car. I'll bring him out."

Chip waited, lying on his back on the hard concrete floor, his heart thumping rapidly like the beat of a trip-hammer. During the night, he had loosened the cords that bound his wrists and ankles, but he had not removed them. He knew he could slip out of his bonds whenever he pleased, but he did not please, for he had made his decision the night before.

He could not fight his way out of the dilemma by sheer brute strength. Only by skill, by trick or device, by the use of his brains could he possibly escape; and so he would make the pretense that he was still firmly bound when the burly man came for him. Even the gag tied about his mouth was still in place.

He felt good. He was not tired. He was, in fact, rested. He had had long periods of sleep during the night. But he was famished, and his stomach growled like a bear demanding to be fed.

Now he heard a key grate in the lock of the door

at the top of the steep stairway. Frank Bristol clumped down the wooden stairs.

"Hungry, kid?" Bristol stood over him.

Chip nodded.

"Okay," Bristol rasped. "I'll take you where I can get some grub into you. You just be a good boy."

Bristol stooped, seized Chip, and lifted the boy to his feet, holding him within the grasp of one powerful arm.

Suddenly Chip saw the swift gleam of the golden pen under his nose! But Chip Power knew exactly what he had to do.

He heard the hiss of gas shooting upward at his nostrils, but he held his breath. Then, closing his eyes, he went limp, pretending to be unconscious.

Bristol lifted him, tossed him over a shoulder like a sack of potatoes, and carried him up the stairs.

Chip's head was behind Bristol's head, so he opened his eyes. He saw nothing that could help him, however. He was being carried through many rooms of an old house, that was all.

Then Bristol opened a door and stepped out into sunshine, and Chip's eyes were closed again. He knew there was another man outside in the car, and it would not do if that other man saw Chip Power's eyes open.

Nevertheless, he blinked open his eyes for one quick look, and in that instant he saw two things. He saw the man sitting in the car. The man had blond hair, but the man's head was averted and he could not see his face. The other thing Chip saw was a sign: CALIFORNIA. Then he was dumped into the trunk of the car, and the metal lid was slammed down.

He heard the motor start, and he was off on his long and uncomfortable ride.

It was hot and stuffy and dark inside the trunk compartment, but there was sufficient air coming through the cracks in the gasket around the trunk lid. *Well,* Chip thought, *at least I won't suffocate.*

Now what?

He slipped out of the cords on his wrists, took the

cords off his ankles, and removed the gag from his mouth. He was cramped, but it was not too bad. It must be a big car, he decided, because the area within the trunk compartment was considerable. There was ample room for him to squirm about.

His outstretched hand touched a round object. It was a flashlight. He lit it and inspected his surroundings. He found a jack handle and took hold of it almost lovingly. At last—a weapon!

It was about a foot long, made of sturdy steel. One end was round, blunt, and strong. The other end was narrow and flat. It would do.

He held on to it for dear life, craftily forming his plan.

When they arrived at their destination, they would open the lid of the trunk compartment expecting to find an unconscious Chip Power. But he would *not* be unconscious! And he would *not* be locked within a stone room in an old house! He would be out of doors!

He would pretend, for those first few moments,

to be unconscious. And then he would slash out at them with his weapon, strike them, if necessary, and run.

Certainly he could not outfight them, but he certainly *could* outrun them!

And then somewhere there would be *people* to whom he could tell his story! No matter what Frank Bristol would say, no matter what the other man would say, he, Chip Power, would have a chance to tell *his* story. The people would call the police, they would call his father, they would call ... anybody ... but Frank Bristol could not pull him away, could not force him away in the presence of other people, normal people, despite the fact that they would be strangers.

He extinguished the flashlight. He lay, knees up, on his right side, the jack handle held close to his body.

The car bumped along many roads.

Then, at long last, it stopped.

Chip braced himself, his muscles tense, waiting.

He heard Bristol's voice: "He's out cold. We've got time."

And the other voice: "For what?"

"We'll walk into town—keep the car here out of sight—and buy some chains."

And the other voice once more: "For what?"

Then Bristol's voice yet again: "What are you, a dope? We'll put chains around him. They'll serve as weights. Then when we dump him in the ocean, he'll stay down a long, long time."

In the dark, hot compartment, Chip clenched his fist more tightly around the jack handle. Tense, frightened, perspiring, he felt a cold shiver despite the heat as he waited, listening.

He heard their footfalls going off, then silence.

He moved. He turned on the flashlight. He used the jack handle, the narrow end wedged into the crack of the lid, as a lever to break the lock. He worked feverishly, trying again and again, pressing all his strength against the lever at the lock, and then finally it cracked open and he lifted the lid.

The sunlight struck him like a blow! He had to close his eyes until he got used to it.

Chip climbed out, sick, faint, hungry, perspiring from every pore. He was cramped, his muscles hurt, and he had to stretch and yawn. Then he tossed the jack handle into the trunk and looked about.

He was in a deserted beach area. He could see the ocean beyond high dunes, gray and gleaming in the sunshine. The car was parked off to a side of a sandy road. He began a slow, dogged trot along the sandy road away from the ocean.

Mouth open, gasping for air, he continued his steady, plodding run for perhaps a mile until he came to an inhabited area. There was a cluster of clean, white-painted houses. He rang the bell of the first one. No answer. He rang again, leaning against the side of the house, panting, sobbing for breath.

The door was opened by a lady with dark skin, dark hair, dark eyes. She took one look at him, became frightened, and tried to close the door, but Chip had his foot in.

"Please," he begged. *"Please!"*

"What—what is it?" the poor woman stammered.

"Please! I need help!"

He could not blame her for being scared. He knew what he looked like—dirty, grimy, sweaty, his clothes wrinkled—obviously a vagrant.

"Please!" he begged and, although he tried to force them back, tears came out of his eyes. "I—I'm not a tramp. Please help me."

The woman hesitated, but studied him. She saw he was a boy, a youngster in dreadful circumstances. She had been warned about vagrants, and she was home all alone, but her heart melted at the sight of the boy trying to force back his tears.

She opened the door.

Chip stumbled in.

She led him into a clean kitchen.

"Sit down," she said. "What's your name?"

"Chip," Chip said. "Please call the police!"

"Police!" the lady repeated, aghast. "Why should I call the police? What is this, anyway?"

"I—I've been kidnapped."

"Oh, *no!* You poor boy!" And now she, too, had tears in her dark eyes.

"Please. Call the police." Chip sat at the kitchen table, clasping and unclasping his hands.

"Look here," the dark lady said, "when did you eat last?"

"Yesterday," Chip said and grinned wanly.

She touched his arm. He stood up. She pointed to a doorway.

"Through that door," she said. "The bathroom. You go in there and wash up. I'll cook up a little something for you. You like bacon and eggs?"

Chip swallowed. "I love bacon and eggs. But— but the police!"

"One thing at a time." The dark lady smiled. "You go and wash up now, hear? What did you say your name was?"

"Chip. Chip Power."

"You go along now, Chip Power. Wash up and come back here."

He washed, cleaned up, came back refreshed to the marvelous odors of cooking, and his mouth watered. She served him bacon and eggs, and buttered toast and jelly. He began to wolf down the food.

"Coffee?" she asked.

He did not like coffee, but this was no time to argue.

"Or cocoa?" she inquired.

"Cocoa, please," Chip said and drank water from a glass she had put on the table. He ate and ate, and the woman watched him and smiled happily. Then she went to a phone on the kitchen wall and dialed a number.

"Hello?" she said into the mouthpiece. "Sergeant Christo? This is Mrs. Brady here. Emily Brady, at Twenty-two Hamilton Street."

"Hi, Emily," greeted Sergeant Christo. "What can I do for you?"

"There's a boy here in my house. He says he was kidnapped."

"*What?*" roared Sergeant Christo.

"That's what he says."

"You sure he's not kidding you?" Sergeant Christo asked. "I mean, if he was kidnapped, what's he doing in your house?"

"It seems he got away. He came here all panting and dirty and practically fell in through the door."

"Did he give you his name?"

"Chip Power."

"Hold the wire a minute, Emily."

"Sure."

When Sergeant Christo's voice came on again, it was deadly serious.

"Emily?"

"Yes, Sergeant."

"Listen, and listen hard. A nine-state alarm came out last night on a missing person. Name: Chip Power. Fifteen years old, tall, blond, blue eyes. Does the description fit?"

"Fits perfectly."

"You just hang on to him," Sergeant Christo

shouted excitedly. "Don't let him leave the house."

Mrs. Brady laughed. "I'm sure he has no intention of leaving. He's practically been begging for the police."

"He'll be getting the police any minute. I've already dispatched a car."

Three minutes later the patrol car arrived, and Chip told his story to two broad-shouldered policemen.

Quickly they rushed him outside and into the patrol car, and they raced along the sandy road to the dunes by the ocean—but Frank Bristol's car was gone!

"Skipped," one of the policemen said. "When they got back here and saw the kid had broken out, they made their getaway."

They rode back, without haste now, to Mrs. Brady's house, and from there Chip called the hotel. The desk clerk gave him Mr. Donovan's number. Chip called and talked to his father and then to Detective Wilson.

"We're all happy you're safe and sound," Detective Wilson said, "but let's get you back to town. You say there's a policeman with you?"

"Yes."

"Put him on, please."

Chip motioned to one of the policemen and gave him the receiver. The policeman listened for a moment, then said, "Yes, sir. All right, sir," and cradled the receiver.

"All right, Chip," the policeman said. "You're on your way home. We'll take you."

Chip thanked Mrs. Brady and went out with the policemen to the patrol car.

It was a long drive, almost three hours, but not unpleasant. For a time they chatted, and then Chip dozed. Finally he was back in New York City and the Hotel Lincoln and suite 903, where he was embraced by his father and an excited Jack, while Detective James Wilson hovered over them, smiling happily.

16 *New Developments*

At the urging of Detective Wilson, Chip swiftly narrated an outline of his adventures all the way from the finding of the wallet in the drugstore to the final call from Mrs. Brady's house.

"Now we'll go into it more deeply," Detective Wilson said. "I'll ask questions, and you answer them as fully as you can. All right, Chip?"

"Yes, sir."

"First and foremost, I want a complete description of Frank Bristol."

Chip described the man.

"No question," Jack declared emphatically.

"That's the same guy who took me."

"Took *you?*" Chip cried. "What are you talking about?"

Jack laughed. "You're not the only one in the spotlight, Brother. It so happens that I was kidnapped, too."

"You were *what?*"

"Easy, boys, easy does it," Detective Wilson quieted them. "We have time, lots of time. But first things first. And first, Chip, I want to get all the details from you. Okay?"

"Yes, sir." Chip grinned. "But I didn't know that Jack also—"

"We'll tell you all about that," said Detective Wilson. "But now, about the house where they kept you, the house with the stone cellar—tell me about that."

"It was by a beach. I could hear the waves swishing."

"There are hundreds of miles of beaches around New York," Detective Wilson informed him.

"Nothing more specific, Chip?"

"Well, I heard Mr. Bristol say on the phone it was a long house, a long beach house—"

And right there came the interruption. There was an imperative knock on the door, and Jack opened it.

It was Lieutenant Cassidy, red-faced and excited, but smiling.

"Jim," he said to Detective Wilson. "I thought you'd be here. I've got big news."

"So have we," Detective Wilson retorted. "We've recovered young Chip Power here."

"Yes, I heard about that. Congratulations."

"Now, what's your news, Lieutenant?"

Lieutenant Cassidy stalked about the room, smiling, triumphant, before he replied.

"Frank Bristol. We developed some fingerprints up there in the apartment on Seventy-second Street, and we processed them through the FBI in Washington."

"Good. Very good!" Now Detective Wilson was

stalking right alongside the lieutenant.

"We learned," Lieutenant Cassidy continued, "that Bristol and another man were arrested and convicted for counterfeiting in San Francisco. The other man's still in jail there, and I had the San Francisco police question him about Frank Bristol."

"Excellent." Detective Wilson was beaming.

"We now know that Bristol is a New Yorker, born and raised in New York, lived most of his life in New York, and we know of some of his favorite haunts right here in New York City. I'm about to go and visit some of those places." Lieutenant Cassidy made a happy little bow toward Detective Wilson. "I was wondering whether you'd like to go along with me."

"You know I would!"

"So would I," Thomas Power declared. "Now that both my boys are home—if I may?"

"Certainly, Tom," said Detective Wilson.

"I'm not finished yet," Lieutenant Cassidy said in a slow, steady tone.

"There's more?" inquired Detective Wilson.

"There's this," murmured Lieutenant Cassidy, and he took a picture from his pocket. "It was wired to us by the San Francisco police."

He displayed the picture to Jack and Chip.

"That's him! That's the guy!" the boys cried.

And now, quite proudly, Lieutenant Cassidy showed the picture to Mr. Power and Detective Wilson.

"Frank Bristol," Lieutenant Cassidy proclaimed. "Now we know exactly whom we're looking for." And he made his happy little bow again. "If we're going, gentlemen, let's go!"

Mr. Power said to Jack, "You're in charge. Take care of your brother."

"Yes, sir, Dad," Jack replied. "Happy hunting!"

17   *Tailing the Suspect*

Chip took a long, hot shower and got into fresh clothes. He and Jack had a bite in the kitchen, and they fed Blaze. Then Jack took Blaze out for a walk. When they returned, Chip said, "Let's talk, Jack. I'm dying to hear all about what happened to you."

Jack looked at his brother in amazement.

"Aren't you tired?" he asked. "I mean, don't you want to take a nap or something?"

"Nap!" Chip scoffed. "I had a long, long night with little to do but sleep. And I slept. And even in the police car, coming back here, I slept. I'm wide-awake and full of beans. Unless *you* want to sleep or something."

"Not me." Jack shook his head. "I'm okay."

"Then, gosh, let's talk. I'm dying to hear, Jack."

They sat together on a sofa and Jack told Chip everything about what had happened to him from the moment Dick Donovan had gone back into his house for the binoculars. He told his story slowly and in great detail. Suddenly he snapped his fingers, his green eyes glowing like emeralds.

"Detective Wilson *said* that in time things would come back to me."

"What?" Chip demanded. "What's come back?"

"That voice."

"What voice?"

"That vaguely familiar voice."

"You mean the voice that said to cut out newspaper type? To arrange the newspaper type—the ransom letter—exactly as he had first written it out?"

"Yes, that voice," Jack said. "Bruce Updyke."

"Bruce Updyke?" Chip queried, squinting, not

remembering. "Who's Bruce Updyke?"

"Mr. Donovan's secretary."

"You must be *crazy!*" Chip jumped to his feet. "Mr. Donovan's *secretary?* Are you sure?"

Jack lowered his head and shook it sadly. "No. I wish I were. I mean—well, it kind of sounded like his voice, kind of high-pitched, you know?" He looked up to Chip, anguish in his eyes. "I—I'm confused. I mean, what would Mr. Donovan's secretary— I mean, what connection between Updyke and Flatnose— I mean, Flatnose, a kidnapper and a counterfeiter?"

"Well, we can find out," Chip snapped.

Jack stirred uneasily.

"About any connection? How?"

"No, not that," Chip explained. "I mean about the voice. You only heard it once. It was when you *knew* it was Bruce Updyke, when Mr. Donovan introduced us. So, let's hear it again. Let's go over there."

"But it's his day off," Jack reminded him. "On

Sunday and Monday he's off, he and the chauffeur. Mr. Donovan told us."

"But Updyke lives in Mr. Donovan's house." Chip looked at his watch. It was ten minutes to eight. "He figures to be home now. We'll kind of drop in, like we're calling on Dick Donovan. We'll work it out for Dick to get Updyke down to us; we'll say Dad gave us a message for him—anything. But you'll hear his voice again, and you'll be able to make up your mind—one way or the other."

Jack was on his feet.

"Okay. We can give it a try. We've got nothing to lose."

Chip patted Blaze, then went to the closet and came back with his strobe camera. Jack regarded it in astonishment.

"Why the camera?" he asked.

"Evidence," Chip replied blithely.

Jack had to smile, shaking his head in wonder. "You can't take a picture of a voice, can you? Now, if you happened to have a portable tape recorder. . . ."

"But I don't. I have a camera." Chip slung the strap over his shoulder and announced, "If you're going to play detective, you take whatever equipment you have. So if worst comes to worst, I'll snap his picture."

Jack burst into laughter, then shrugged. Chip had been through a terrific ordeal. Why argue?

"Okay," he said. "Let's go."

"What about Blaze?"

"We'll leave him here."

They went out into a night flooded with moonlight. They walked swiftly the short distance to the Donovan house. Suddenly Chip grabbed Jack's arm.

"Look!" he whispered.

Bruce Updyke was walking down the steps.

"He's sure a sinister-looking guy," Chip whispered. "I mean, those dark-tinted glasses."

"Look, if a man needs dark-tinted glasses, he needs dark-tinted glasses. That doesn't mean he's sinister."

"Well, I only said . . ." Chip muttered lamely.

"Just don't be prejudiced, little brother."

"Not me. Never. I'm not prejudiced. And watch out who you call 'little.' "

Bruce Updyke turned left, walking toward Fifth Avenue.

"Move," Chip urged his brother. "Don't just stand there. We're tailing him."

"Okay, Detective Power," Jack said politely. "We're tailing him."

18 *A False Lead*

But the boys were disappointed.

Bruce Updyke led them on no merry chase, and he took them to no secret place. Mr. Updyke strolled to Fifth Avenue, turned left, walked to 34th Street, and entered the Empire State Building.

They watched from across the street as Updyke rang the night bell and was admitted. They could see through the glass doors as he signed the night book and entered the elevator.

"Big deal," Chip said forlornly. "The Empire State Building, where Mr. Donovan has his office. Mr. Updyke's gone up to do some evening work."

"So am I going up there!" Jack exclaimed.

"But, Jack—"

"I'm going to talk to him. I'm going to hear his voice. Well, Chip? Get a move on!"

They crossed the street and rang the night bell of the towering building. A man in uniform opened the door.

"Yes?" he inquired.

"I have to see Mr. Updyke," Jack said, "at the Donovan Advertising Agency."

"He just got here," the man said and led them into the lobby. "Donovan Agency—twenty-eighth floor." He pointed to the night book. "Sign in, please."

Jack signed his name, where he was going, and the time.

"How about you?" the man asked Chip.

"I'll wait down here," Chip replied.

The man took Jack into the elevator, and they disappeared.

With nothing to do while waiting, Chip snapped

a closeup picture of the open book.

Then the man came down, smiled at Chip, and went about his work.

Chip waited, looking in the store windows of the lobby floor. In a few minutes there was a ring in the elevator, and the man went up again and came down with Jack. He opened the door for them, and they went out again in the moonlight and began walking back to the hotel.

"Well?" Chip asked.

"I told him we were out for a walk on Fifth Avenue and we happened to see him going into the building. I told him I came up to ask him if there were any new developments in the kidnapping— *my* kidnapping, which was supposed to be Dick Donovan's."

"So?" Chip queried.

"He was very nice, very cordial. He didn't bawl me out for interrupting his work—"

"But what about his *voice*?" Chip demanded.

Jack shook his head without enthusiasm.

"It sounds similar, but I wouldn't swear."

"Look, maybe you ought to call Detective Wilson."

"What would I tell him?" Jack asked desperately. "I can't *swear* it was his voice. A lot of voices sound alike. I can't swear, I'm not certain, I'm not sure—I just can't make myself ridiculous accusing a man because he has a voice. . . ."

They were at the hotel. They rode up to 903 in silence.

Blaze awoke from a nap, greeted them, and went back to sleep.

"I'm hungry," Jack announced.

"Me, too," Chip said. "But hold it a second."

"What now?"

"I've got some work to do." Chip grinned mischievously.

Jack went to the kitchen to do the cooking, while Chip became busily engaged developing the picture he had taken.

Jack opened a can of soup and prepared meat

patties. Soon Chip came in waving a photograph.

"Here, take a look," he said.

Jack viewed a photograph of the open night book from the lobby of the Empire State Building, a page of signatures including his own.

"So, Detective?" he scoffed. "So you took a picture of my signature. So what?"

"Not your signature. *His!*" Chip declared triumphantly.

"Whose?"

"Your possible suspect, Bruce Updyke."

"Oh, brother! I was talking about his *voice,* remember?"

"Well, I'm talking about his handwriting," Chip insisted.

Jack frowned in pure bewilderment.

"What's his *handwriting* got to do with it?"

"Listen," Chip begged. "You say the voice is similar. Right?"

"Right."

"Well, suppose on top of that we can pin his

handwriting to the handwriting on the kidnap note. . . ."

"Brother, are you dumb!"

"I am?" Chip inquired mildly.

"The kidnap note was on a sheet of paper with pasted-on letters cut out from a newspaper."

"But what happened up there in the house in the Bronx?" Chip insisted. "You told me yourself. The guy with the voice, the vaguely familiar voice, had first written out the note. Then the other guy was supposed to copy it by pasting on those words from newspaper type. Didn't you say that when you told me the story?"

"I did."

"Well, the fellow with the voice had to first *write* that note. He *wrote* it!"

"So what?" Jack demanded helplessly.

"So now we have a specimen of his handwriting to compare!"

"Oh, no!" Jack groaned. "To compare to *what?* Everything up there was burned in the incinerator after I escaped. No trace of anything. I told you. Don't you remember?"

Chip closed his eyes and nodded sadly. "Yes, I'm afraid I do remember." Then, opening his bright blue eyes, he gamely added, "Well, it was a good idea, wasn't it?"

"Brother, let's eat!"

"That's a good idea, too," Chip said.

19   *"Ready, Willing, and Able"*

Jack and Chip ate, washed the dishes, and went back into the living room.

"Well, so much for Bruce Updyke," Chip sighed.

"Yeah—but what about your other guy?"

Chip's eyes narrowed. "What other guy?"

Jack sat in an easy chair, Blaze beside him. Stroking Blaze's head, Jack talked slowly, musingly.

"Up there in the Bronx, I heard three of them. Somewhere out near a beach where they held you, there were two of them. Now, both of us, for sure, had Flatnose—Frank Bristol. So far so good?"

"Yes," Chip acknowledged.

"Now, I didn't see either one of the other two. But when you told your story to Detective Wilson, you said you *did* see another one. Let's take a crack at working on that," Jack said hopefully.

Chip shook his head. "No good. Bristol was carrying me over his shoulder. Outside, I opened my eyes for one quick look. I saw that sign that read 'California,' and I saw a guy sitting in the car next to the driver's seat."

"Well, what did he look like?" Jack asked.

"I couldn't see. His face was turned away. He had blond hair—period. Next thing I knew I was being dumped into the trunk of the car."

Jack compressed his lips. It seemed he and Chip were being thwarted at every turn. But he kept at it stubbornly.

"Look," he suggested. "Detective Wilson was going to cross-examine you. You know, dig in for information, pry out details. Okay, so then Lieutenant Cassidy barged in, and off they all went on more immediate business. So—suppose I play Detective

Wilson. I'll ask the questions, you'll answer. How about it, Chip? Let's give it a try."

"Sure," Chip agreed. He sat down on the floor beside Blaze, crossed his legs, and looked up at his brother. "Shoot, Detective Wilson," he chuckled.

Jack crossed his arms and looked down sternly.

"All right," he intoned solemnly. "You heard Mr. Bristol say on the phone it was a long house, a long beach house. Now, when did this phone conversation happen?"

"Last night."

"Any idea to whom he was talking?"

"It's my guess," Chip ventured, "that he was talking to the accomplice—the blond guy who came out to help him today."

"And why would that be your figure, young man?" Jack asked, imitating Detective Wilson.

"Simple," Chip replied. "He said something about getting rid of him—meaning me—tomorrow morning—meaning today—and then he said, 'Okay, I'll see you in the morning.'"

"Very good," Jack applauded. "And what else did they say?"

"Not 'they,'" Chip corrected. "I only heard one side of the conversation."

"Okay, what else did *he* say?"

Chip knitted his brows, trying to recollect.

"Well, he said something about checking out of there for good. . . ."

"Meaning the apartment on Seventy-second Street. And we now know why—the counterfeit bill you had given the cab driver. He realized it could be traced back, just as it was. If he'd stayed at that apartment, the cops would have already nabbed him by now. But so far," Jack protested, "I haven't heard any mention of a beach house."

"Oh, I remember that part distinctly," Chip said. "It was just when the phone rang, right at the beginning. 'Yes, this is Frank,' he said. Then he said, 'I've checked out of there for good . . . . Yes, I'll be right here by the long beach house . . . . '"

Suddenly Jack leaped to his feet.

"Wait a minute! Hold it! Hold everything!"

"What—what is it?" Chip gasped.

"Long beach house!" Jack danced about wildly, Blaze barking and jumping after him. Now Chip stood up, and Jack clutched his sleeve. "The long beach house! It may have nothing to do with *long*— with *length!* There's a city near New York, a beach resort—Long Beach! *The house in Long Beach!*"

And now it was Chip who was dancing about, Blaze leaping and barking after him. The poor dog looked at the brothers as though they had gone crazy.

"Jack, I think you've got something there!" Chip cried. "Could be! Could be!"

"And that sign you saw," Jack exclaimed. " 'California.' "

And now Chip subsided, squinting to understand.

"But what's the name of a state got to do with it?"

"It could have been a street sign," Jack yelled. "Was it?"

"I—I don't know. I just got a glimpse. The name of a state. California."

Jack tried to hold back his bubbling excitement. "There are plenty of streets named after states. It could have been California Street or California Avenue. No? Yes? What? Hey?"

Chip's eyes were wide with admiration.

"Maybe you really *ought* to be a detective," he beamed.

Jack darted to the telephone. He dialed Information for the number of the Long Beach Post Office. He got the number and called it. A tired voice answered:

"Long Beach Post Office. We're closed now. Only the night crew is on."

"Could you please tell me whether you have a California Street out there?"

"Yes, we have," the weary voice said. "Now, what is it? What can I do for you?"

"You've done it," Jack said triumphantly. "Thank you very much."

He hung up, his own eyes wide in wonder now, gazing at Chip.

"Well?" Chip whispered.

"Yes," Jack said.

"Yes, *what?*"

"Yes, there *is* a California Street out there."

And now they were like statues, silent, frozen, staring at one another, both of them frightened. This was no longer a game. It was real!

"L-Look," Chip stammered. "Call Detective Wilson."

"You bet," Jack said.

He dialed police headquarters and asked for Detective James Wilson.

"Sorry, he's not here now," said the voice at the other end.

"May I leave a message?"

"Sure."

"Would you please tell him that Jack Power called? Tell him—please write this down—that the house where Chip Power was held is on California Street in the city of Long Beach. Do you have all that?"

"Yes."

"And tell him that Chip and Jack Power are going out there right now. Thank you."

Jack hung up and remained motionless.

Eyes bulging, Chip goggled at his brother.

"We—we're going out there?" Chip asked, his scalp prickling with the pins and needles of excitement.

Jack tried twice before he recovered his voice.

"Don't you want to, Chip?"

"I—I don't know. Don't you think we ought to wait for Detective Wilson and Dad?"

"No."

"But why not?"

Jack rubbed his palms against the sides of his trousers.

"Because Flatnose is liable to clear out of there, just as he cleared out of his place on Seventy-second Street."

Chip considered that and came up with an answer.

"But he took me far away—all the way to Montauk. He said that on the phone: *'We've got to get rid of him, but not here, not near this house—far away from here.'* So why should anybody be suspicious of the house in Long Beach? Why should he want to clear out of there?"

"Who knows?" Jack exclaimed. "You *did* escape. Could be he'll get scared off from there, too. Chip, we've got a red-hot lead, but if we let too much time go by, it can cool off. It could be we're all wet on this, but I say we should give it a try. Unless— unless you don't want to go."

"I do." Chip's face was a study in perplexity. "Oh, I do, Jack! But—but—Dad. I mean. . . ."

"I know he'll understand," observed Jack, but with a degree of uncertainty that Chip missed. "Chip, we've got to give this thing a go, but unless it's unanimous, unless you vote with me, then we just sit here and wait. How do you vote?"

"Honest, I want to vote yes. But—"

"It's up to you," Jack sighed. "My vote is in."

And now Chip's grin was wide and happy. "Me,

too. So's my vote in. Yes! There's just no other way."

"We'll be careful. You just promise that, Chip."

"Sure."

"No crazy chances."

"I'll be good," Chip promised.

"Okay, get your jacket." Jack got his own jacket and laughed. "And *don't* bring your camera. The most we'll need is a flashlight."

"How about money?"

"I've got plenty of money." Jack pocketed a flashlight. "Ready, Chip?"

"Ready, willing, and able."

20   *"The Long Beach House"*

They boarded the train at Pennsylvania Station. They had learned by inquiring that the trip would take about fifty minutes. They had purchased magazines, one for each of them, and several bars of candy.

Comfortably settled on the train, they munched candy, their eyes glued on the magazines. Neither of them knew what they were reading, but they preferred to pretend, not wanting to talk.

They felt guilty. They both knew that they were off on a dangerous adventure, and they were uncertain if their dad would approve. Without wanting to, without desiring it, they had already given him a great deal of trouble and worry during the last two days. This time, any trouble would be of their own making.

Their purpose was good—they knew that. They meant well—they knew that, too. But they did have lingering doubts. Should they have had patience? Should they have remained at the hotel and waited for their father? Should they have waited for Detective Wilson?

No! Once they had worked it out, once they had solved the riddle, how could they just sit and wait? Once they had made their great discovery, then it was a time for action! Oh, they would be careful, but when opportunity knocked they just couldn't sit home and let it fly by! Furthermore, they had left a message at headquarters for Detective Wilson telling where they were going.

And so they sat there pretending to read, not talking.

And then the train entered the terminal, and the

conductor pulled open the door of their air-condi-
tioned car and called, "Long Beach! Last stop!
Long Beach! All off!"

Here it was cooler than in the city. The stars
overhead seemed brighter, and the moon was round
and white in the spangled sky.

They walked toward a taxi stand.

"Could you take us to California Street?" Jack
asked the taxi man.

"California and where, young fella?"

"California—and—and the main street," Jack
replied.

"Sure. Hop in."

It was not a long ride.

The taxi stopped. They paid and got out.

"Which way is the ocean?" Chip asked.

"That way." The taxi driver pointed to the left;
then the cab pulled away and the boys were left
alone.

They walked slowly along dim sidewalks toward

the ocean. They walked with thumping hearts. They walked as though they were on a narrow precipice, but the knowledge of each other's presence helped to stifle their fright. A little salt breeze sprang up from the ocean, cooling the perspiration on their faces. They could hear the low, ceaseless moan of the sea.

They were getting closer. The sound of the ocean was louder.

And then they were on the last block. There were just a few dark houses, and then a long gap with no houses at all. Finally they were at the end, by the ocean, and there on the last corner was one single, solitary house.

They stood still and listened. They could hear the swish of the waves on the sand.

"This must be it," Jack whispered.

It was an old, seedy, flaky house.

Chip squeezed Jack's arm, then let go and pointed.

Right there on the corner outside the house was the street sign: CALIFORNIA STREET.

Jack nodded. "Keep your fingers crossed," he whispered.

The white light of the moon gave an eerie illumination as they walked silently around the house, inspecting. The windows were shuttered, the doors boarded-up—except one door in the rear.

Jack tried the knob. The door was locked.

Then they heard a sound that sent their hearts up to their throats. It was a rapping sound, a knocking sound, and they stood stock-still, listening intently.

It sounded like some ghostly woodpecker pecking away at some object in the night.

Chip's hair stood on end. He leaned very close to his brother. "What—what is it?" he whispered, his voice quivering.

The tapping came from the side of the house facing the sea.

Jack drew a deep, long breath. "Let's go find out," he whispered.

Carefully, very carefully, shuffling on tiptoe, they

made their way to the side of the house by the sea. There it was dark, the moon in the sky hidden by the upper stories of the old house.

Jack switched on the flashlight. The round white beam scurried up and down the wall of the house like some lost, luminous, frightened spider, and then came to rest on the shutter of a window on the ground floor.

The shutter was loose, the gentle wind from the sea tapping it against the frame of the window.

Chip's sigh of relief burst from his throat like an explosion.

"Quiet!" Jack whispered. He pulled at the loose shutter and pried it open, but the window was locked.

"Hold the flashlight," he said softly to Chip, who took it. "Now point it down."

Chip did as he was told. Jack found a rock on the ground.

"Now shine it up at the window," Jack whispered, and the light returned to the window.

Jack tapped the rock against the window beneath the lock and broke the pane. He dropped the rock and carefully inserted his hand through the jagged hole. His fingers found the catch inside, and he turned it. Then gently, slowly, he withdrew his hand through the circle of pointed edges of sharp glass.

Then he stood still for a moment, catching his breath.

"You okay?" Chip whispered.

"I think so."

"You didn't cut yourself?"

"I hope not."

"Stick out your hand."

Jack put out his hand. Chip turned the light on it. There was no blood.

They smiled in the darkness, then Jack lifted the window.

He took the flash from Chip and climbed in. Then he turned and helped his brother in, their fingers intertwined. Jack noted that Chip's hand was ice-cold, but he noted at the same time that his own hand was, too.

"Okay?" he breathed.

"Okay," Chip murmured.

Jack lowered the window, but the breeze came through the broken pane and made a hollow, rustling sound in the dark room.

Jack shivered, then played the beam of the flashlight into the room.

It was an old, badly furnished, musty, smelly room. The paint was peeling from its walls.

"Recognize it?" Jack whispered.

Chip had had his eyes open when Bristol had carried him out.

"I think so," Chip replied in a muted tone, "but I'm not sure. Let's look some more."

They followed the long beam of the flashlight through other rooms of the old, rotting house, the floors creaking and screeching beneath their feet— and then Jack jumped to Chip's touch on his arm.

"Wha—what?" Jack said.

"This is the house. Definitely."

"Good boy."

"Then let's get out of here," Chip whispered.

"You bet," Jack said. "Mission accomplished. Except—"

"Except what? What now?"

"I want to call it in to police headquarters. I want to tell them this definitely *is* the house." Even though Jack spoke in a whisper, a thin ghostly echo came back at them.

"What's the sense of that?" Chip asked. "Detective Wilson's probably on his way already."

"Probably," Jack said. "But he doesn't know that this is the right house, just as we didn't know. Now . . . ."

"But," queried Chip, "if he's already on his way, how can you call him?"

"They've got those two-way radios," was Jack's whispered reply. "I call it into headquarters, and then they'll relay the message by shortwave. There must be a phone here somewhere."

"That there is," Chip agreed.

"Okay, you just follow along after me. I'll make the call, and we'll get out of here. We'll wait around somewhere by the main street. Now you just stay after me, kid."

The beam of light in front of him, Jack shuffled through more rooms along creaking floorboards, bare and cobwebby. Suddenly the flashlight discovered a black phone on a white metal table.

"Okay. Here it is."

He turned to Chip.

No Chip! *He was alone in the room.*

"Chip," Jack called guardedly. "Chip!"

No answer. Nothing but ghostly echoes.

He retraced his steps back into the next room, and then he heard Chip's voice.

"Jack!" It was a whisper, an urgent whisper.

Of course. Here in this house, Chip wouldn't yell.

The beam of the flashlight scanned all about the room. No one! No Chip!

"Jack! Where are you?"

It seemed to come from below.

Now he played the beam along the dirty, dusty, rotten floor—and then he saw the hole.

Chip had fallen through the rotted floor!

Jack pointed the beam of light down through the hole, and there, a long way down, he saw Chip standing in a stone basement room.

He lay out on the floor and put his head in the hole, flashing the beam downward. Chip was smiling up at him.

"Are you hurt?" Jack called.

"Not me," Chip asserted proudly. "I know how to fall. I went limp and took the shock on all fours. I'm okay."

"Catch," Jack commanded.

He tossed down the lighted flashlight. Chip gathered it in like a fly ball to the outfield.

Then he shone the light up and Jack could see what to do. He lowered himself into the hole, his fingers holding the floorboards at the edge of the hole, and then dropped lithely into the basement room.

He took the flashlight from Chip.

"Move!" Jack said.

Chip moved about, waving his arms, jumping up and down, to show he was okay. He had no pain, no broken bones.

"Good, great," Jack sighed in relief, and now he flashed the beam around the stone room. There was a steep wooden stairway with a door at the top. "Is this the room where they kept you?" he asked.

"No," Chip replied. "But it was a room like this one. This must be the next-door basement room. Jack!"

"What?"

"*Look!*"

In the dark, stone room, Jack flashed the beam to where Chip was pointing.

In a corner of the room there was a printing press on a huge metal table, and there were steel plates alongside it.

"The press to make the counterfeit bills!" Chip exclaimed. "Oh, brother, have we got them dead to rights now! I wish Detective Wilson were here."

"Let's get out of here," Jack growled.

"Yeah, but how?" Chip demanded.

"Up those stairs and out that door," Jack promptly declared. "I'm sure it's not locked. No reason why it should be. There's no prisoner down here—like there was in the next-door basement room."

"Like I said," Chip grinned, "you really *should* be a detective."

At precisely that instant the room was bathed in brilliant light. Someone had clicked a switch at the top of the stairs!

The boys' heads jerked upward simultaneously.

The door at the head of the steep wooden staircase was wide open, and two men stood in the doorway!

Chip recognized one of them instantly. The man holding the thick black gun that was ominously pointed down at them was Frank Bristol!

The other man was tall, blond, broad-shouldered, and for a moment Chip drew a blank. Then he knew him. It was Mike Cheever—Mr. Donovan's chauffeur!

"Well, well, the trouble boys," rasped flat-nosed Frank Bristol, grinning evilly. "How do you like that, Mike? *Both* of them. Hello, boys—and good-bye!"

The hand holding the gun became rigid, but Mike Cheever grabbed at the outstretched arm. "No. Not here," Cheever said.

"You're so right, Mike," Bristol rasped. "I'm glad you stopped me. I almost lost my head." And then his gritty voice called down to the brothers Power, "Okay, you two. Up! Up these stairs! And one false move out of either of you, and you're dead! Do you hear me? *Dead!*"

"Do as the man says," Jack quietly advised his brother.

"You!" Bristol shouted.

"Me?" meekly inquired Jack.

"That's right! You! Drop that flashlight!"

"Yes, sir," Jack said and quickly dropped the flashlight.

"Okay! Now move! Up the stairs, trouble boys!" He and Cheever moved back to give the boys room to come through.

Even now as they went up the stairs, Jack was thinking. Mike Cheever! Why had neither he nor Chip recognized *his* voice, had never felt it to be even faintly familiar?

And then he remembered.

When Mr. Barry Donovan had introduced his secretary and his chauffeur, the chauffeur had never acknowledged the introduction by speaking. *He had merely smiled and nodded. They had not heard Mike Cheever's voice in Mr. Donovan's home!*

And now they were up the stairs, being prodded by Bristol's gun.

Mike Cheever led them out into the pale moonlight of the street.

A big car gleamed in the wash of the moon.

"Okay, get in the back, you two," Frank Bristol commanded. "Mike!"

"Yes, Frank?"

"You drive!"

"Mike!"

"Yes, Frank?"

"Not Montauk, this time. This time, we'll go in the other direction. We'll take them out to the Rockaways."

"Yeah. Smart," Cheever grunted.

Cheever climbed into the driver's seat and started the motor. The boys sat in the rear, Frank Bristol alongside, his black gun menacing them.

"Okay, Mike, let's go," Bristol rasped.

The car had to be turned around. It was pointing toward the ocean, and Mike Cheever had to maneuver it, up and back in the street, until it was pointing in the other direction—and that direction, Jack thought, meant the destruction of himself and his brother. He would have to do something. He would not sit and wait, unresisting, to be killed by

Flatnose and his big, black gun. Perhaps, somewhere, when they came to a stoplight. . . .

And then great headlights pierced the gloom,
blinding them, and two cars hurtled down the street,
blocking their exit. Mike Cheever braked shriek-
ingly, and policemen were running out of the other
cars, and Cheever and Bristol were running away.
There was the crack of pistol fire and the command:
"Halt!"

Cheever and Bristol stopped dead in their tracks,
their trembling hands in the air, and their hands
were brought down by uniformed policemen and
manacled into handcuffs.

And then Mr. Power was holding his sons in a
tight embrace and Chip was sobbing, "Dad . . . this
is the house. . . ."

And Detective Wilson was saying, "Easy, boys,
easy does it. All your troubles are over. It's all over
now. We've got time, lots of time. You did good
work—great work—great work indeed. . . ."

21   *Confined to Quarters*

After thorough investigation of the house in Long Beach, the police transferred the culprits to headquarters in New York City. But all questioning was suspended awaiting Detective Wilson, who was in suite 903 of the Lincoln Hotel intently listening to Jack and Chip explain how they had worked out the location of the house and all that had happened to them up to the time they were saved by the police.

"Good, good, excellent," beamed Detective Wilson. "A beautiful piece of police work. You have my compliments, both of you."

"Thank you," Chip said uncertainly, looking sideways at his father.

Mr. Power's expression was mixed. A part of him looked pleased, a part of him looked displeased.

But Blaze was entirely pleased with all the company he had. His tail kept wagging and he went from one person to another, nudging his head at their hands to be petted.

"Poor Blaze. He's been awfully neglected of late," Jack remarked.

"Let's not change the subject," Mr. Power advised. "In one way I agree with Detective Wilson, but in another way I stoutly disagree. Yes, you boys *did* do a smart piece of work, but it was *not* your work to do. You took a terrible risk."

"But we did call headquarters first," Jack said.

"And then you should have stayed right here," Mr. Power admonished.

"But, Dad," Chip put in, "it was really like a scouting expedition. You know?"

"Scouting!" Mr. Power scoffed.

"We just wanted to be sure it was the right house," Chip explained. "And then all we were going to do was keep an eye on it—on anyone coming or going —until you folks arrived. No risk, really, Dad. What risk?"

"*What risk!*" Mr. Power exploded. "No risk at all—except there you were in that car with the muzzle of Bristol's gun pointing at you both."

"Well . . ." Chip began. His eyes slid to Jack, whose eyes were steadfastly cast down upon Blaze, whom he was petting.

But Detective Wilson came to their rescue. "Bygones are bygones, and all's well that ends well," he philosophized. "Let them be, Tom. They did do a good job, and they're entitled to a good, long rest now."

"If only they *will* stay put and rest," said Mr. Power, but he could no longer repress his smile. He was proud of his sons.

"Oh, yes, sir, we'll stay put and rest," Chip said, grinning.

"Yes, sir, we'll do that," Jack agreed.

"All right, then, Tom," said Detective Wilson. "Would you like to come downtown and sit in on the questioning of the prisoners?"

"I'd love it," replied Mr. Power.

"How about us?" cried the irrepressible Chip. "We'd love it, too."

His father looked upon him sternly.

"That's just about enough of that," said Mr. Power.

"Yes, sir, Dad," Chip murmured contritely.

"Now, remember, you boys stay put," Mr. Power warned, his smile in his eyes now, and then he and Detective Wilson departed.

"Gee, I'd have loved to be in on the finish," Chip grumbled.

"Me, too," said Jack. "But Dad's had just about enough of our gallivanting around. Furthermore, it's late."

"Grown-ups!" Chip complained. "Gosh, I wish I were already grown up."

"And the grown-ups say just the opposite," Jack remarked. "They all say they wish they were young again. How about some hot chocolate?"

"Fine," exclaimed Chip. "And there's apple pie in the refrigerator."

They had their snack in the kitchen and enjoyed every morsel. Afterward they sat around for a long time chatting about their adventures of the last couple of days. And then, once again in the living room, Jack, looking at his watch, said, "Maybe we ought to go to bed."

"I'm not the least bit sleepy," Chip offered.

"Me, neither. And look at old Blaze."

Blaze was romping around as if it were mid-afternoon. He had had a long rest. He was full of energy, bounding about, looking for action.

"Where's his ball?" Jack asked.

"Search me," Chip replied.

But Blaze had found a substitute for his ball. He had nudged open the closet door and now he brought a shoe to Jack. It was one of the shoes Jack had worn

the wet and rainy night he had escaped from the house in the Bronx.

Jack tossed the shoe for Blaze to retrieve it.

"Maybe we ought to take him out for a walk," Chip suggested.

"Hey, Blaze, bring back the shoe," Jack called. "Look at that dog. What's the matter with him?"

Blaze was eagerly worrying the inside of the shoe. After a few moments he pulled something out and brought it in his teeth to Jack. It was the folded paper that Jack had inserted as a makeshift inner sole to cover the nail hole and protect his wounded foot that rainy night.

Blaze sat in front of the easy chair in which Jack was sitting. The folded paper lightly held in his mouth, Blaze looked up at Jack, his glowing eyes begging his young master to take the folded paper from him.

So, idly, Jack obliged the dog.

He took the paper from Blaze's mouth, casually unfolded it, looked at it disinterestedly—and then he sprang from the chair, high in the air, as though catapulted.

"Wow!" he shouted.

"What? *What?*" Chip cried in amazement. "What's going on?"

But Jack was at the phone dialing police headquarters.

"Detective Wilson, Detective Wilson," he yelled into the mouthpiece. "Connect me with Detective James Wilson."

"Hold on, please," answered the voice at the other end.

Jack waited, shifting from foot to foot.

Then the voice said, "He's not here."

"Not *there!*" Jack exclaimed. "He *must* be. I know he's with two prisoners—Frank Bristol and Mike Cheever."

The voice came alive. "Who is this?"

"My name is Jack Power. As a matter of fact, my father's with Detective Wilson right now—Mr. Thomas Power."

"Jack Power," said the voice in a tone of admiration. "We've heard about you and your work down here tonight."

"Thank you," Jack said quickly. Then he went on urgently, "Where is he—Detective Wilson? And my father?"

"Ordinarily, we wouldn't give out that information," the voice chuckled. "They went up with the prisoners to Donovan's house. You know Donovan?"

"Yes, sir, thank you." Jack hung up and yelled to Chip, "Get your picture."

"What picture?" exclaimed Chip. "What in the world has gotten into you?"

"The picture of the book! The picture you took in the Empire State Building! Now quick! Hurry up!"

And so with picture and paper and Blaze on a leash, they walked quickly through the moon-washed streets toward the house on 32nd Street.

22 *Charges and Countercharges*

Dick Donovan, clad in pajamas and bathrobe, opened the door to Chip's ring. His eyes rounded like saucers when he saw who the late-night guests were.

"Well, hi," he said, a crack in his voice registering his amazement.

"Hi," Jack said uneasily. "What're you doing up so late?"

"What do *you* think?"

"Are they here?" Jack said, grinning.

"You bet," was Dick's rejoinder. "Big goings-on. What are *you* fellows doing up so late?"

"Taking Blaze for a walk," Jack replied dryly.

"Yeah," Dick drawled. "Taking the dog for a walk," he chortled. "You want in on the excitement, don't you?"

"You bet," Jack admitted. As they stepped into the foyer he inquired, "Where are they?"

"In the living room," Dick told him.

"Do you think we'll be intruding?" Chip asked.

"Sure," Dick conceded. "But—so what? You're entitled. From what I've heard so far, you guys have been the heroes of the whole affair."

They were in front of the living room door.

Dick inhaled deeply, shrugged, then opened the door, and all three with Blaze marched in.

Jack took a quick look about, and the first thing he saw was his father's frown of disapproval. Looking away from his father, he took in the scene.

Uniformed policemen stood at the sides of the room like sentinels. Mr. Power was seated, and so was Mr. Barry Donovan, who, like his son, was looking very upset indeed.

In the center of the room stood Detective Wilson, Frank Bristol, Mike Cheever—and Mr. Bruce Updyke, neatly dressed in a dark suit and white shirt.

Jack opened his mouth to speak but was silenced by his father's upraised hand.

"Hush!"

Suddenly all eyes were on Jack.

Meekly Jack sat in a high-backed chair. He removed Blaze's leash and laid it on the floor. Blaze curled up beneath Jack's chair, made himself comfortable, and left the wrangling and arguing to the humans. Blaze was not interested.

Chip sat with Dick on a sofa.

Detective Wilson had a small smile for the newcomers and then a grim look for Frank Bristol.

"Yes, please go on," was his command to Bristol.

"Well, like I said," rasped the flat-nosed Bristol. "Those twenties the kid found in my wallet were bad counterfeits. We were never even going to try to pass them."

"Then why," demanded Detective Wilson, "did

you have so many of them in your wallet?"

"I'd brought them from the house in Long Beach," retorted Bristol. "They were lousy. I was going to put them in my vault here in the city."

Hands folded behind his back, Detective Wilson paced about the room, then stopped and pointed a finger at Mike Cheever.

"Okay, you now. Cheever. Your turn."

Muscles quivered in Cheever's jaw. He ran his fingers through his blond hair. He sighed, then spoke.

"Frank told us—"

"Frank?" Detective Wilson interrupted and pointed at Bristol. "You mean him? Frank Bristol?"

Now Jack saw another policeman in a chair in a corner, taking down all that was being said in a notebook.

"Yes, Frank Bristol," said Cheever.

"Go on, Mr. Cheever. Continue."

"Well, Frank told us that with fifty thousand bucks he could buy new plates and new equipment in Mexico that could fix up our printing press perfect. We could improve those counterfeit twenties so they'd pass anywhere. If we could put together fifty thousand bucks, we could earn ourselves a cool million, and then pull out of the country before any trouble started up. And that's when Bruce Updyke presented his brilliant idea to us."

"He's lying! He's a liar!" shouted Bruce Updyke indignantly.

Detective Wilson whirled to Updyke.

"Do you deny knowing Frank Bristol?"

"No," exclaimed Updyke. "No, I do not deny knowing him. We were all born and brought up in the same neighborhood here in New York—Frank, Mike, and myself. What I *am* denying is this story they made up between them." Updyke adjusted his dark-tinted glasses. "Sure," he said. "They want to get off easy, so they arrange this story to make *me* the mastermind of the plot."

"*He's* the liar!" snapped Bristol. "Not me. Not Mike. We're telling the truth!" He pointed a thick, accusing finger at Updyke. *"His* idea, *his* suggestion—all of it!"

"It's the truth, so help me!" Mike Cheever interposed. "It was his idea—Bruce Updyke's!" Cheever sank into a chair, lowered his head into his hands, then looked up with haggard eyes. "He laid it out for us, all clear and simple," Cheever muttered. "We would kidnap Dick Donovan, we would get the fifty thousand from Mr. Donovan, and we'd buy that equipment in Mexico. With me and him right here in the household, we could convince Mr. Donovan to pay out that dough without calling in the cops. Bruce Updyke carries a lot of weight with Mr. Donovan; he has a lot of influence here. Doesn't he, sir? Doesn't he, Mr. Donovan?"

"Yes," Mr. Barry Donovan replied, "I'm afraid I put too much confidence in my personal secretary."

And now it was Frank Bristol shouting: "And if worst came to worst—they—Mike and Bruce right here in the house—they would know just what was going on. They would know if and when any cops

were called in. We really had it made!" he exclaimed. "Coming or going, we had it made. Two of our group right here in the house, knowing everything that was going on—from the *inside!*"

Cheever bounded to his feet and went to Jack. "So Frank picks up this one, the wrong kid, and we wind up with trouble after trouble." He laughed bitterly. "We wind up with a double kidnapping and nothing to show for it but trouble." Cheever sighed and crossed to Updyke. "Now the least we can do is tell the truth." He poked at Updyke's shoulder. "His idea! All his idea! All!"

"That's a lie!" Updyke screamed. "A dirty lie!"

"The truth," snorted Bristol contemptuously.

"Lies! Lies!" Updyke protested loudly. "A pack of lies—all of it! They've joined together in a plan to get off easy! By accusing me—by making *me* the mastermind—then they become only foolish accomplices." He stood up straight and tall and rather graceful. "Well, I challenge them!" He looked about. "I challenge you all! Proof!" he demanded belligerently. "I appeal to Mr. Donovan. Where's the proof—except the statement of these two self-admitted criminals?"

Sagely, slowly, Mr. Donovan nodded.

"He does have a point there, Mr. Wilson."

"He has no point at all!" exclaimed Jack Power.

All eyes, at once, turned upon him. A cascade of questions, many and overlapping, enveloped him. The din in the room was tremendous.

"Quiet! Quiet!" ordered Mr. Power.

And then there was a hush, a heavy silence, and Jack Power was the center of all their attention.

Jack's tongue flicked out at his dry lips, wetting them. He swallowed and tried to compose himself, thinking where to begin. The silence weighed down upon him.

"When they had me up there," he finally stammered, "up there in the house in the Bronx, there were three of them in another room talking. The voices came from a distance away, but one stood out, vaguely familiar—Bruce Updyke's."

"Were you sure?" asked Mr. Donovan.

"No."

Quite kindly and quite fairly Mr. Donovan said,

"I'm afraid that isn't very substantial evidence."

Jack nodded. "I agree," he admitted.

"He heard the voice again. Tonight," Chip chimed in. "Tell them, Jack."

"Easy, son," Detective Wilson cautioned Chip.

"Yes," Jack explained. "I visited with Mr. Updyke this evening in the office of the Donovan Advertising Agency. In the Empire State Building."

Barry Donovan glanced toward Updyke.

"So he did," said Updyke with no trace of discomfiture.

Jack rubbed his jaw. "My reason, my purpose, was to test out his voice. It was sufficiently similar—well —at least to make me suspicious."

"So?" queried Detective Wilson. "How did you make out?"

"It still sounded like the voice up there in the Bronx—the voice of the man who had said he had written out a note to be copied in newspaper type."

"The ransom note," Chip shrilled.

"Now, Jack," entreated Detective Wilson. "This

is important. Would you swear that Updyke's voice *was* that voice in the Bronx?"

"No," Jack admitted. "Otherwise you'd have heard from me. But, please, there's more. My brother."

"Chip?" inquired Detective Wilson.

"He stayed downstairs in the lobby when I went up to talk with Mr. Updyke. He had his strobe camera with him. He took a picture of the night book."

"Night book?" questioned Mr. Donovan, his forehead wrinkling.

"Where the people sign in," said Jack. "Show them, Chip."

Chip brought the picture to Detective Wilson. Mr. Donovan stood up, and he and Detective Wilson examined it together.

"There you see Mr. Updyke's signature," Jack declared. "His handwriting."

"You needn't have gone to all that trouble," Updyke sniffed haughtily. "I'd be happy to volunteer a specimen of my handwriting."

"You *did* volunteer a specimen of your hand-writing," Jack informed him.

"I *what?*" said Updyke.

"He *what?*" exclaimed Mr. Donovan.

"Easy does it," Detective Wilson said, trying to calm everybody.

Jack took the folded paper out of his pocket and unfolded it. He held it tightly while he said, "Up there in the Bronx when I crashed down the door and broke out, I got a nail through the sole of my shoe. I picked a sheet of paper out of the trash basket, folded it, and put it in the shoe to cover the hole. Actually, I forgot all about it, but tonight Blaze dug it out and brought it to me. I think it's a pretty good sample of Mr. Updyke's handwriting. I'm sure it'll check out against his signature."

In a fury, Updyke lunged savagely at Jack. "Let's see that!" he cried fiercely.

But Mr. Power, instantly on his feet, pulled Updyke away.

"Not yet," Jack said, smiling, "but soon, I hope. Mr. Donovan?" he called.

"Yes, young man?"

"The ransom note. Do you still have it?"

"Right here." Donovan took it from the mantel-piece.

"It's remained here with my permission," said Detective Wilson.

"Would you both please look at it?" Jack suggested.

Donovan shrugged, Wilson smiled, but they complied, somewhat reluctantly, as though giving in to the whim of a slightly daffy youngster.

And now Jack read from the sheet of paper in his hand:

" 'If you want your son back, prepare fifty thousand dollars in unmarked bills. If you call in the police, you will never see your son alive. We will be in touch with you.' "

Jack was reading from his sheet of paper the very same words that Donovan and Wilson were reading from the pasted-on newspaper type.

"Good heavens!" growled Barry Donovan, looking up, staring in utter amazement at Jack Power.

Jack fluttered the sheet in his hand.

"I took it out of the trash basket while they still thought they had me, before they burned the contents of the trash basket in the incinerator. It's the original handwritten note."

Bruce Updyke made one last desperate lunge, but Mr. Power intercepted him, and then the uniformed policeman took Updyke in tow.

Detective Wilson compared the handwriting on the note with Updyke's signature on Chip's photograph.

"Identical!" he announced.

There were no further denials from Bruce Updyke.

24 *"Unfinished Business"*

The room resounded with exclamations of congratulations on a case well solved, and then Bristol, Cheever, and the crestfallen Updyke were hustled out by the policemen and Detective Wilson.

A semblance of quiet and order descended upon the living room of the house on 32nd Street.

"Gee whiz!" exclaimed Dick Donovan, and somehow that summed it all up.

"Once again, my congratulations," Mr. Barry Donovan offered. "Thomas, you've every right in the world to be extremely proud of your boys."

Thomas Power's dark eyes glowed. "I am," he

said quietly. "Very much so."

Chip yawned sleepily.

"I think it's time to take them home now and tuck them into bed," Mr. Power said, chuckling.

"Bed?" queried Chip. "Who's sleepy?"

That produced a hearty laugh from everyone.

"I am," said Dick Donovan.

"Me, too," said Jack.

"Not me," said Chip drowsily.

"Time to go home, boys," said Mr. Power.

"Just one moment," interposed Mr. Donovan.

"Yes, Mr. Donovan?" inquired Thomas Power.

"There's a bit of unfinished business," observed Mr. Donovan. "The small matter of a check—which I'm going to write without further delay."

"Check?" queried Mr. Power.

"I'm a man of my word, sir," replied Mr. Donovan. "I offered a five-thousand-dollar reward, and young Jack Power certainly earned it. Who else but Jack caused the apprehension of the mastermind of this entire affair?" And as though in answer to himself he added, "No one else *but* Jack."

"Oh, no, thank you, sir," Jack said.

"You'll share it with your brother, of course."

"Thank you again, but I'm afraid we must both refuse," Jack declared. "Right, Chip?"

"Right," Chip agreed. "It was Blaze."

"Correct," said Jack. "It was good old Blaze that turned the trick, not us. And what would Blaze do with a cash reward? Blaze's money is love and affection, and when it comes to that, Blaze is a millionaire. Right, Blaze?"

Blaze wriggled out from under Jack's chair, barked once, pranced happily, and waved his tail in agreement.

THE POWER BOYS

Whitman CLASSICS

Black Beauty	The Call of the Wild
Tales to Tremble By	Tom Sawyer
Heidi	Robin Hood
Tales from Arabian Nights	The Wonderful Wizard of Oz
Mrs. Wiggs of the Cabbage Patch	Robinson Crusoe
Little Women	Wild Animals I Have Known
Huckleberry Finn	The War of the Worlds

Here are some of the best-loved stories of all time. Delightful ... intriguing ... never-to-be-forgotten tales that you will read again and again. Start your own home library of WHITMAN CLASSICS so that you'll always have exciting books at your fingertips.

Whitman ADVENTURE and MYSTERY Books

Adventure Stories for GIRLS and BOYS...

New Stories About Your Television Favorites...

REAL LIFE STORIES
To Dance, To Dream
The Great War
Heroes in Blue and Gray

POWER BOYS SERIES
The Haunted Skyscraper
The Flying Skeleton
The Burning Ocean
The Million-Dollar Penny
The Double Kidnapping

DONNA PARKER
In Hollywood
At Cherrydale
Special Agent
On Her Own
A Spring to Remember
Mystery at Arawak
Takes a Giant Step

TROY NESBIT SERIES
Forest Fire Mystery
Indian Mummy Mystery
Mystery at Rustlers' Fort

I Spy

Lassie
Secret of the Summer
Forbidden Valley
Wild Mountain Trail

The Man from U.N.C.L.E.

Combat! The Counterattack

The Beverly Hillbillies

The Munsters
The Great Camera Caper
The Last Resort

Gilligan's Island

The Big Valley

Bonanza

Voyage to the Bottom of the Sea

Walt Disney's Annette
Mystery at Medicine Wheel
Mystery at Moonstone Bay
Mystery at Smugglers' Cove